YESTERDAY ONCE MORE

Amy Jones is all set up to be married. But then unexpectedly her ex-lover and father of her five-year-old twins marches unexpectedly back into her life, unleashing memories of love and betrayal. To Zach Morgan, the twins' existence is a complete shock. He'd no idea Amy was pregnant when she'd abruptly ended their affair and run away, refusing all contact. Can he convince her he'd never intended to break her heart, that he still loves her and wants to marry her?

Books by Sarah Evans
in the Linford Romance Library:

LOVING AUNT LOU

SARAH EVANS

YESTERDAY ONCE MORE

Complete and Unabridged

LINFORD
Leicester

First published in Great Britain in 2007

First Linford Edition
published 2010

British Library CIP Data

Evans, Sarah.
   Yesterday once more.- -
   (Linford romance library)
   1. Single mothers- -Fiction. 2. Love stories.
   3. Large type books.
   I. Title II. Series
   823.9'2–dc22

   ISBN 978–1–84782–983–2

Published by
F. A. Thorpe (Publishing)
Anstey, Leicestershire

Set by Words & Graphics Ltd.
Anstey, Leicestershire
Printed and bound in Great Britain by
T. J. International Ltd., Padstow, Cornwall

1

'Tasty!' said Amy's friend, Linda, and she wasn't referring to the iced buns they were serving for the village fayre's afternoon teas.

Amy glanced up and studied the back view of a tall, powerfully-built man in snug black jeans. 'Hunk,' she said. It was a game they'd played many times before. Linda was constantly searching for her ace alpha male.

Amy, on the other hand, wasn't.

'Front view's even better,' said Linda. 'An absolute dreamboat.'

Amy finished serving her customer with a smile and a friendly comment before tossing a second glance across the gloomy green expanse of the tea tent. The cowboy-booted stranger with his shock of black wavy hair was now heading towards them.

The breath suddenly caught in Amy's

throat. Her heart began to do a dramatic drum roll. The blood fizzed in her veins and made her dangerously light headed.

But it couldn't possibly be Zach Morgan? Not after all these years.

And he was getting closer. Any moment now, they would be face to face. Amy clenched her fists so her nails sliced into her now damp palms. Would Zach recognise her? Probably. Definitely!

She suffered an agonising moment of indecision. Should she stay or should she do the cowardly thing and run? Self-preservation won out. She dived for cover under the white servery tablecloth and hid.

'Two teas, please. One white, one black.'

Amy shut her eyes and bit her knuckle. His voice hadn't changed. It was deep, honeyed and sexy, with an underlying Australian twang. It used to make Amy's toes curl with desire when he'd whispered words of love. And now her toes were curling again.

This time in fright. She huddled further under the table. Linda could serve the tea. No way was Amy going to show herself. She peeped out from under the starched tablecloth as soon as she reckoned it was safe.

'Has he gone?'

Linda rolled her eyes. 'Yes. So what's with the disappearing act, hmm? Suddenly developed an aversion to drop-dead gorgeous guys?'

'Something like that. He has definitely gone?'

'Yes, Amy. So what's going on?'

Amy crawled out of her hiding place and shoved a strand of hair the colour of sun-bleached straw behind her ear. She gave her peasant-style skirt a brief shake to dislodge the blades of grass adhering to the bright material.

'Amy?' Linda prompted.

Amy sighed and pulled a face. 'It's complicated.' Why now? Why today after six years of utter silence?

'How complicated is complicated?'

'Very. Where is he now?'

Linda gestured across the tent. Amy looked where Linda's finger was pointing and suffered a lightning bolt straight through her body.

Because Zach, who was standing with the daughter of one of Amy's employees, was staring straight at her as if he'd seen a ghost. Amy saw his lips move, framing her name.

'Amy?'

She spun around and as fast as she could, deaf to everything but the panic drumming in her ears and Zach shouting her name. She fumbled with the stiff lacing of the tent. She broke a nail as she yanked the canvas apart, flipping it back so that she could wriggle through the narrow gap.

The sudden exposure to the dazzling sunlight blinded her, but not for long. She ducked under the guy ropes and began to run.

She sprinted towards the nearest group of people. Hopefully she could lose herself in the crowd.

4

Again she heard Zach call her name. She quickened her pace. What had brought him here? She'd never, ever expected to see him again. He should be in Australia, not here at her village fayre.

Then she had a nasty thought. Goodness, he wouldn't be looking for her, would he? No, of course not. He wouldn't have waited this long if he'd wanted to see her again.

Unless he wanted to see the children?

No! Not that. He didn't deserve them. Hadn't earned the right to meet them.

Dodging past several people, Amy searched around in desperation for an escape route. She had to hide. She couldn't spend the rest of the afternoon high tailing it around the village green with a six-foot plus hunk in hot pursuit.

Amy ran past an assortment of sideshows and ducked down a side alley into the next row of small tents. She dashed headlong into one that was shrouded in multi-coloured floaty scarves and had

5

Gypsy Fortunes emblazoned in sparkly red paint over the doorway.

The gypsy tent was empty except for a striking redhead who was sitting at a small table draped in purple velvet and hunched over an upturned goldfish bowl. She was clothed from head to toe in black with artistically draped Indian cotton shawls and chiffon scarves.

Umpteen brassy bangles jangled half way up her arms and heavy, intricately fashioned chains adorned her neck. Thick theatrical make-up completed the spectacular job of Gypsy Bethany Rose.

'Want your fortune told, luvvie?' she cackled. 'Just cross my palm with gold and I'll tell you what's in store, my pretty.'

'Beth, darling, I haven't got time to mess about. I need your help.'

'Sounds interesting. Wait while I change into my fairy godmother costume and flex my wand.'

'Beth! Please, be serious. I've got to escape from him. Hide! Oh my goodness, what shall I do?'

'I'll consult my crystal ball.' Beth giggled and peered into the upended fish bowl. Its usual inhabitants were having a vertical holiday experience, swimming in a vase on the kitchen draining board at Beth's home.

'Beth!'

'OK, OK, just joking. Why don't you slip out the back of the tent and I'll try to stall whoever it is that's after you.'

She waggled her kohled eyebrows questioningly, hoping for a clue as to who the pursuer was. Amy didn't oblige. She was too busy scrabbling underneath the canvas.

Once through to the other side, Amy dashed towards the large flower marquee. Surely she'd be able to hide in there?

A surge of adrenaline rushed through Zach as Amy darted through the gap in the tent. He'd found her! He quickly strode to the servery and vaulted over it.

He was oblivious to the rash of raised eyebrows from the village tea drinkers.

Wrenching back the marquee canvas, he was forced to waste valuable seconds loosening the webbing further to accommodate his large frame, before squeezing through.

Once outside the marquee, he whipped his head from side to side. Where had Amy gone? Which direction? He scoured the thronging crowd many of whom were dressed to complement the fayre's country theme. Then a sudden flash of bright skirt caught his eye.

There! There she was, threading through a large group of people who were cheering on some sort of tug-o-war contest. She immediately disappeared into a small tent.

Zach wasn't far behind her. He forcibly flung back the curtained door of *Gypsy Fortunes*, causing a tinkling shower of hundreds of tiny brass balls.

'Amy?' His eyes adjusted to the dark interior. Where was she? Where had she gone? 'Sorry, I thought I saw Amy Jones run in here,' he said to the woman at the table.

Beth sucked in an appreciative breath and hammed it for all she was worth. 'Cross my palm with gold, sonny, and I'll tell you . . . ' she said.

Zach took a step back in surprise. 'Excuse me?'

The woman appeared to sink into a deep trance, sighing gustily and then intoning, 'I see a beautiful blonde, green-eyed woman crossing your path . . . there will be many, many obstacles to overcome. Many trials, many problems, many, many ups and many downs and . . . er . . . many interesting things . . . but she will bring you . . . aaahhh . . . ' Beth dramatically rolled her eyes and sibilantly hissed through her teeth.

In spite of himself, Zach's attention was riveted by the bizarre performance. 'What?' he asked when she'd finally stopped hissing.

'Aaahhh!' Beth resumed enthusiastically, waving her arms about like an overzealous banshee, wafting exotic Eastern perfume about the tent. 'Aaahhh . . . aaahhh . . . ' Abruptly she stopped and cocked an eye at the handsome stranger. 'Cross my palm with gold and I'll tell you,' she said with a grin.

'The — !' Zach muttered a few gypsy curses himself at being sucked in by her act.

Zach flung some coins down on the table. 'I don't suppose you're going to tell me where Amy went?'

'Sorry, no can do,' said Beth. 'Gypsy oath of silence.'

Zach left the tent abruptly, the bells jangling brassily once more. He scanned the crowded fayre. This time he was out of luck. He couldn't see Amy anywhere. She'd gone.

Zach returned to the tea tent where Melanie Philpot was still waiting with barely concealed annoyance. 'So you finally decided to come back,' she said.

The tea sat in front of her, stone cold and unappetising.

He forced a smile. 'I'm sorry, Melanie.'

'I'm sure you had a perfectly good reason for chasing Amy Jones, though I can't imagine what.'

'You know Amy? That's great.' He experienced a sudden leap of interest in the woman who, until now, he'd found intensely irritating.

'We don't move in the same social circles, if that's what you're implying, Zach. She's our house cleaner.'

Amy was a cleaner? What had happened to all her dreams of university? Teaching? Travelling?

During their intimate moonlit walks along romantic French beaches, Zach recalled how they'd shared their visions of the future. He wondered why she'd not pursued them. Maybe he'd find out by the end of the day. If he was lucky enough to catch the elusive Ms Jones.

* * *

The heat was suffocating. Amy swiped at her perspiring brow. Her thin cotton top stuck to her back. The smell of warm, damp mud and grass tickled her nose.

She'd taken refuge under one of the long display tables in the flower tent. Safe behind the endless metres of white cloth, she sat hunched and miserable. She'd been foolish to run at the first sight of Zach. She hadn't done anything wrong.

She should have stood her ground and brazened out the meeting. After all, what could he do to her now? Face it, a lot!

Because there was the children to consider. And her sanity.

So perhaps she had been right to bolt and hide rather than face the man who'd broken her heart and left her pregnant.

Caution and commonsense had always ruled Amy's life. The only exception was when Zach Morgan was thrown into the equation. And then, boy, didn't things go haywire. The only time she'd followed her heart rather than her head she'd ended up in a heap of trouble, which had had on-going repercussions.

Not that she would change anything.

She loved the twins to bits, but it hadn't been easy becoming a single mother at the age of eighteen.

Seeing Zach again had sent a pack of emotions roaring through her. Not least shock, panic and anger. But also a fatal curiosity that was best left unsatisfied if she knew what was good for her.

Amy began to feel calmer. And the calmer she became, the more confident she felt. She really didn't have to skulk in dark corners to avoid Zach Morgan. She was a grown woman. What could he possibly do to her at such a public event as the fayre? She was surrounded by family and friends. She was being ridiculous.

That decided, she poked her head out from under the cloth.

Whoa! She reared back as if stung, all her sudden confidence gone in a flash. Zach was in the tent. And with the insufferable Melanie Philpot fawning at his side. Amy liked and respected Melanie's parents, Audrey and Henry, but Melanie treated her as if she was plagued with a socially unacceptable disease. Amy had the grace to admit, the feeling was mutual.

It was typical, thought Amy, that Zach had become involved with Melanie. She was similar to that beautiful French sophisticate, Chantelle, whom she'd discovered clasped in Zach's arms on that fateful August day.

So he was still running true to type. Hah! She wasn't surprised. Not one jot. His love affair with Amy had been a fleeting aberration. She'd been the morsel of wholesome rough to spice his usual expensive smooth taste. How galling. How deflating to the ego. But at least it strengthened her resolve to have nothing to do with him.

Amy heard Zach and Melanie approaching her table. Amy's heart thundered in her ears. They stopped immediately in front of her hiding spot. She could just see their shoes peeking under the tablecloth. If her heart thudded any louder the whole tent would be privy to her panic.

Amy rolled her eyes. It was typical of her luck that she'd hidden under the one table exhibiting Henry Philpot's roses. Any other table and she would have been safe.

'These roses smell heavenly.' Melanie breathed in the heady perfume of the deep red Ena Harkness blooms. 'Daddy always sweeps the boards at these village shows. His roses are far superior to anyone else's.'

'Mmm.' Zach's preoccupied response made Amy grin. He would have to learn to sound much more enthusiastic if he wanted to endear himself to Melanie.

As Melanie chattered on about the trophies her father had won over the years, Amy listened with growing impatience. She wiggled her cramping toes to keep her blood circulating. Her calf muscles began to knot painfully. She stifled a groan and madly massaged her leg. If Zach and Melanie didn't walk on in a second, she'd be writhing in agony at their feet, which was not something to look forward to.

But still Melanie carried on her monologue. Amy's leg was going into spasm. Well, if they wouldn't move, then she would have to before her muscles seized up completely. She got down on all fours and began to inch along the damp ground. Her hip accidentally clipped one of the trestle table legs as she manoeuvred herself. The trestle shuddered.

The roses in their presentation vases shivered and one velvet petal fell on to the stark white cloth, staining it like a drop of scarlet blood.

Zach absently watched the roses tremble again. Two more petals spilled on to the cloth. Zach narrowed his eyes as an audacious idea struck him. No, surely not? But Amy was nowhere else in sight. It was worth a try.

He whisked back the linen and ducked down. A colourfully clad bottom was rapidly disappearing up the opaque green, trestle-legged tunnel.

2

'Zach, what are you doing?' Melanie's startled exclamation was ignored. Zach was already flinging the cloth back in place and striding swiftly up the aisle to the head of the table. Zach and Amy reached it simultaneously.

As Amy warily lifted the cloth to check if it was safe to come out, Zach's hand flew out and clamped around her wrist. She gave a shriek.

'Got you!' he said with grim triumph and hauled her unceremoniously to her feet.

Frantically, Amy tried to pull herself free, but the iron band of his fingers wouldn't give. 'Let me go!'

'Why? So you can race off again. I don't think so. I've had enough of tearing about the fayre for one day. You can just hold still for one minute and talk to me.'

She gave one last, hard tug and then grudgingly gave up, breathing deeply to try and regain her composure. She didn't really want to draw attention to their confrontation. She had the children to consider. And Rob . . .

'Why did you run as soon as you saw me, Amy?'

'I should think that was obvious.'

'Not to me. Why?'

'I don't have to answer to you, Zach Morgan. I'm my own woman.' Her chin tilted in pugnacious challenge, her eyes held his steadily.

He didn't immediately answer. His gaze slid over her in a thorough assessment that caused Amy's blood pressure to rocket and depleted her meagre stock of self-confidence.

'I agree,' he said, and his voice changed timbre. It was suddenly a soft, seductive burr. 'You look every inch a woman.'

The honeyed warmth of his compliment momentarily unbalanced Amy. But only for a split second.

18

He still found her attractive — too bad. That was his problem, not hers. She wanted nothing to do with the low-down, cheating rat who had shattered her dreams and broken her heart six years ago.

Amy raised her chin another belligerent notch. 'Thanks for the compliment, but I don't care a fig what you think of me, Zach Morgan. I haven't cared for years. My life has moved on. You mean absolutely nothing to me, so quit these bully-boy tactics and let me go!'

He didn't. Instead, Zach lifted his free hand and twitched the low scoop neck of her blouse back in place. The unexpected touch sent fork lightning through Amy's nervous system.

'How dare you!' She yanked the top up even higher. Heat surged through her. Whether it was anger or something dangerous, she didn't dare analyse.

Amy gibbered in frustrated rage at his proprietary arrogance. But before she could yell at him, she was frozen by the arctic tones of Melanie Philpot.

19

Amy could have kicked herself. How could she have forgotten the ice maiden?

Melanie glided up to Zach and attached herself to him like a barnacle on a ship's bottom.

'Zach, really,' said Melanie. 'Leave the woman alone. You're causing a scene and it's blatantly obvious that she doesn't want anything to do with you.'

Zach's dark slate eyes meshed with Amy's. A question vibrated between them. Another surge of heat coursed through Amy and she was horribly sure that a telltale blush was staining her cheeks.

No! She denied furiously, silently, her eyes warring with Zach's. No! She did not want him. That was long over between them. Buried deep, if not forgotten.

Zach raised one eyebrow. A smile danced around his lips and eyes. Amy almost groaned out loud. He didn't believe her! How mortifying.

'Zach,' said Melanie. 'I'm bored with

all this. Let's go and find my parents.' She slipped her arm through Zach's to lead him away, but Zach disengaged her hold, keeping his full attention on Amy.

'Don't think you've seen the last of me, Amy Jones. It's no accident I'm here. This is only the beginning.'

Amy shivered. What did he mean, only the beginning? What did he want of her?

Zach kissed the tips of his fingers and pressed them firmly over Amy's lips. The unexpected gesture zapped another electrical charge through her body, leaving her blood fizzing and popping. Heavens, just his fingertips evoked a tumultuous response in her.

It was a relief when Zach and Melanie left the tent. Amy needed the respite. Her emotions were jangling. She still didn't have a clue what Zach was doing here. Did it really matter what had brought him? He was here and causing trouble, that was the bottom line.

She decided to check on the twins

before returning to her neglected post in the tea tent. Moving stiffly through the fayre ground, her legs working like jerky clockwork, she felt all out of kilter. Zach's shock reappearance in her life had thrown her completely. She would have to pull herself together for the children's sake.

As Amy neared the coconut shies, a smile softened her worried countenance. Luke was shouting out in true fairground style with his 'roll up, roll up' routine as he helped some of the older boys from the local primary school run the stall.

Her heart swelled with pride. He was a good boy, always cheerful and eager to join in things. He loved working on the shies, but as Amy drew closer, her smile slipped and her heart gave a tremendous, painful lurch. It thudded hard against her ribcage and then almost stopped.

Because there was Zach Morgan. He hadn't gone off with Melanie after all. No, he was picking up some little wooden balls, handing over money, laughing and joking — with his son!

Shock paralysed her.

She was unable to move, unable to breathe, consumed with fear as circumstances unravelled rapidly beyond her control. Had Zach realised he was talking to his son? Amy anxiously nibbled her lower lip. Maybe he hadn't. Maybe if she slipped away, he'd never realise the connection.

She took one last squint at the man and boy laughing together. She prayed their encounter would be brief and uneventful and then spun on her heel to leave.

'Mum!'

Amy shut her eyes in despair! Too late. She hadn't been fast enough. Luke had seen her. Perhaps, if she ignored him, he wouldn't persist.

But Luke had other ideas. 'Mum! Over here!'

Amy gave up. She turned back. Luke was waving at her enthusiastically. Weakly, Amy waved back. She had an awful premonition of doom and wasn't disappointed as Zach turned to see who Luke was calling to. When he realised it was Amy, he immediately stiffened. He said something to Luke who grinned and nodded.

'Hey, Mum! Come and have a go at the coconuts. This man said he'd pay for you.'

This man is your deserting father, Amy wanted to shout out loud. Instead, she forced a tight, polite smile.

'How kind,' she said and wished that she was safe and far, far away with the children. The next few minutes could be disastrous. She had to play it cool. If Zach still hadn't recognised his son, there was a chance he never would . . .

Zach held out three wooden balls towards her. She took them, making darn sure that her fingers didn't brush his as he popped them in her hands. She wasn't ready for another lightning shock. Not for a long, long time.

She eyed up the rows of hairy-husked coconuts and imagined one as Zach's head. She pulled back her arm and threw her whole weight behind the ball. It hurtled through the air and mashed the coconut to smithereens. Shell and coconut milk flew in all directions.

Amy savoured a satisfying, if juvenile, sense of achievement.

'Oh, wow, Mum! Way to go.' Luke hopped from one foot to the other and punched the air. 'That was wicked. You usually miss completely.'

Zach's eyebrows zipped to his hairline. 'Not bad. Not bad at all.'

Amy tossed him her remaining two balls. 'See if you can match it,' she challenged.

He did. Effortlessly. Toppling first one coconut and then another. He executed a mocking salute. 'Anything you can do . . . '

'Want to go again, Mum, and see if you can do it a second time?' Luke interrupted, tugging on Amy's arm.

'No, darling. I'll quit while I'm ahead.' In more ways than one. She had to get Zach away from Luke. This situation was much too dangerous to prolong by playing games.

'OK, I'd better choose you a coconut then.'

'I'll give you a hand,' said Zach.

Man and boy stood side by side as they discussed the merits of the various coconuts, Luke wanting to select the very best for his mother. Amy's heart contracted sharply. Man and boy, father and son. Grey eyes met grey eyes and Amy's heart bled at the reflected likeness.

A surge of panic engulfed her. She was pushing her luck. She must separate them, now, before Zach realised.

'How old are you, son?' Zach asked, tousling the boy's dark hair.

Amy gritted her teeth. Now they were on dicey ground. She had to do or say something, anything, to salvage the situation. But her brain refused to work. She opened and shut her mouth. Not a squeak. Her vocal cords were on strike too.

'Five,' Luke disclosed with innocent cheerfulness. Amy squeezed shut her eyes. Despair washed through her. Now they were in deep, deep trouble.

'Five!' The word exploded from him. Zach rounded on Amy.

Amy cleared her throat, trying to dislodge the hard lump of pain that was preventing her from speaking. Her voice came out a croak. 'Please, Zach! Not here. Not now.' She didn't want him launching a full-scale inquisition in front of Luke. She had to protect her son.

Zach hesitated. Emotion was roaring through him. He'd been shocked when he'd discovered Amy had a child. Selfishly, he'd hoped she was still single and unattached. So much for revisiting past loves. So much for long fostered dreams.

But he was even more shocked that the boy was five.

He glanced back at Luke, who was joshing with his school friends, and Zach frowned. His mind whirled. 'He can't be five.'

'He is.'

Zach glanced at Amy's waxy white face and knew it was true, that she'd gone straight from his arms into those of someone else. The idea appalled him. He refused to accept that Amy would have formed another relationship so soon after jilting him. So did this mean she was married?

'I can't believe it!' His voice was strangled.

Amy laid her hand fleetingly on his arm. 'Please. Let it go. Don't say anything more.' She prepared to leave. 'I have to get back to the tea tent,' she said. 'I'm sorry . . . '

'Amy! Talk to me.' He needed answers, but he spoke to Amy's fast retreating figure.

Zach's frown deepened. He looked again at the boy. He had dark hair that was almost the same colour as his. And the big grey eyes, they were similar too.

Something moved deep within him as another, more startling possibility faced him. And the more he stared at the small boy, the more the possibility hardened into something tangible and absolutely amazing.

'Amy! Wait!'

She didn't. She was actually running now, her rainbow skirt swirling around her slim legs. Zach sped after her, his long strides quickly closing the distance between them. He caught hold of her arm and hauled her around to face him.

'I think you have some explaining to do!' he said.

3

'No!' She attempted to yank her arm from his vice-like grip. Her stomach began to roil. She felt sick and angry. Zach Morgan had no right to march back into her life and set everything on edge. Dear Lord, she didn't want him here, foisting himself on her and the children, upsetting their life, spinning it into turmoil and confusion.

'No!' She wrenched again. Zach's grip tightened. Tears of long buried hurt and frustration welled in her eyes. She blinked them away. She wouldn't show him how vulnerable she was. She mustn't. If ever she had to be strong it was now.

'Hell, Amy, you have to talk to me. I need to know.' His own frustration flowed out of him and settled around her like a suffocating cloak. 'Tell me what's going on. What have you been hiding from me all these years?'

'Nothing!' How dare he accuse her of such a thing!

'Don't lie to me, Amy. Is the boy mine?'

He didn't know? Could that possibly be true? Amy almost wept in relief. She could deny he was Luke's father and everything would be all right again.

But would it? Who was she fooling? She had notified Zach about the twins' birth not long after they were born. He knew all right.

Zach gave her a short, sharp shake. 'Is he my son?' he demanded.

'You're hurting me.' She winced.

He immediately let go. 'I'm sorry. I didn't mean to. But I need to know, Amy. Dear heavens, I had no idea . . . '

'Mummy, I'm starving. Can I have something to eat?' A high-pitched, little girl's voice interrupted them. Oh, no, it was Emma. That was all Amy needed. 'Can I, Mummy? Please?' Emma nestled up to her mother's side, winding her arm around Amy's waist.

'Of course, poppet.' Amy stroked her daughter's dusky mop of curls and hoped she sounded normal, but there was a nervous quaver in her voice. 'We'll go and find something at the tea tent.' She braved a glance at Zach. He was rooted to the spot, staring at the child as if he had seen a ghost.

Of course, once again there was no mistaking the family likeness. The dark, slate grey eyes, straight black brows and raven-black, curly hair. Luke and Emma weren't identical, but it was obvious they were twins. And it was also blatantly obvious whom they took after.

'Twins?' The question cracked into the frigid silence.

Amy's chin notched up defensively. He was doing a great performance of being surprised. In fact, he looked as sick as she felt. Good. Let him suffer too. It was about time.

He read her silence as affirmation. 'Twins! Why didn't you tell me?' His voice rose in accusation.

Amy spluttered, 'Why?'

He might as well have dropped a lighted match into a full can of petrol. Amy's wrath whooshed up in flaming magnificence, her eyes flashing fiery green, her cheeks flooding with bright crimson, her lips thinning to a tight, scarlet line as self-indignation fuelled her wrath.

She launched herself at him, furiously jabbing her forefinger into the muscular rigidity of his broad chest. Her words tumbled out, tripping over themselves in a glorious release of anger that had been too long suppressed.

'You have the audacity to ask me that! I did tell you, Zach Morgan. I wrote as soon as I first found out I was pregnant. I wrote when I had the twins. I prayed that I would hear from you, that you would come, if not for my sake, for the children's. But did you bother? Oh, no! You'd already moved on and found someone else. How many were there, hmm? How many other foolish, naïve girls who fell for your good looks and charm? And how long did that little French minx survive? Probably longer than me with all her sophistication and artifices.'

'I presume you mean Chantelle?'

'Of course I mean Chantelle. Who else!'

'I married her,' he said quietly. The stark admission acted like an icy drench of Amy's furious tirade. It immediately quenched the white-hot fire as she absorbed the appalling implications.

'You married her? Oh, Lord.' She clutched Emma to her side, burrowing her fingers into the child's soft curls, and tried to exercise some control on her see-sawing emotions. She didn't want to upset her daughter and she didn't want to lose her complete cool in the public domain of the fayre in front of her family and friends, but she felt very close to doing so.

'Why did you have to come here?' she whispered as tears spilled down her cheeks. She wiped them away, mad at herself for showing weakness. 'Why have you come here, Zach? What's your real reason if you claim you knew nothing of the children?'

'To find you.' He sounded exasperated, as if the reason was obvious.

'I find that hard to believe. You wouldn't have left it for so many years if you'd really wanted to see me again.

'You didn't even bother to reply to my letters.'

'What are these letters you're referring to? I received no correspondence from you. If you'd written to me, Amy, I would have come. You have to believe that. Pregnancy or no pregnancy, I would have come. It crucified me when you jilted me in France without a single word of explanation.'

'You expect me to believe that? Dream on! You didn't want to know, Zach Morgan. You didn't want the responsibility and complications of being saddled with a pregnant eighteen-year-old girlfriend. Chantelle was a much better bet.'

'Amy, I'm not lying to you. I never

received any letters. When you first ran away, I was going to come after you, but I had to leave France immediately. My father had suffered a stroke and was in intensive care. I had to go home as soon as possible.'

The timing had been awful. All Zach had wanted to do was race after Amy and find out what was wrong between them and make it right. But, of course, his first concern had been his father. At the time, he'd presumed he would return and smooth things out with Amy, but things hadn't worked out like that.

'Dad died and I had to take over the grape growing and winemaking. I was suddenly saddled with huge responsibilities. I had a lot to learn and worked long hours. There was never the chance to come and find you.'

'So what happened to my letters?'

'I don't know, Amy. But I swear, I never saw a letter from you.'

'I wish you'd never come.'

'Amy!'

'I have to get back to the tea tent. I'm already late.' She stumbled past him as if drunk, still holding Emma tight to her side.

'We must talk,' said Zach, reaching out and lightly touching her arm.

Amy flinched. 'Must we? What's the point, Zach?'

'You know we have to. I'll come and see you tonight.'

'I don't want to ever see you again.'

'I'm not walking away, Amy. We have to get this sorted.'

4

'Sweet tea is good for shock. And you sure look as though you've had one.' Linda grinned when Amy made it back to the tea tent and settled Emma into a chair to eat a scone smothered in jam and cream.

Linda handed Amy a cup and then plonked her hands on her hips and cocked her head to one side, watching Amy through narrowed eyes.

Beth, who was taking time out from her fortune telling gypsy stall, was waiting excitedly for Amy to take a sip before blurting out, 'Are you going to end the suspense and tell us who that incredibly sexy man is?'

'As if you haven't already guessed,' said Amy bitterly.

'We have a fair idea.'

'So he is the twins' father?' Linda prompted.

Amy dipped her head back in her hands and moaned a muffled yes.

'Oh, Amy, how . . . ' Beth grappled to find the right word. She and Linda had been privy to Amy's heartbreak in the early years. They'd been free to go off to university and travel while Amy had been grounded with the twins. It hadn't been easy being such a young single mum, even with the love and support of family and friends.

'Frightful,' Amy supplied for her. How else could it be described? Her life was tumbling around her ears. She could lose Rob and possibly have to share custody of the children with Zach, which could mean them leaving the country. She clamped down on a sudden surge of panic.

'No, not frightful,' Beth protested. 'Amazing! He is absolutely gorgeous.'

Amy looked pained. 'Where is the loyalty of the sisterhood!'

'Face it, Amy, he's a walking bombshell.'

'I agree,' Linda pitched in. 'No

wonder you succumbed to the boy if the man is anything to go by.'

Amy sighed. 'Zach Morgan is a force to be reckoned with, I freely admit to that. But there is another factor to be taken into consideration which rather cancels out everything else.'

'Which is?'

'He's married.'

'Oh, Amy,' said Linda, surprise and sympathy in her voice. 'Are you sure?'

'He married the French girl he'd been two-timing me with all those years ago.'

'Oh, luvvie,' said Beth, enveloping her in a big hug. 'I'm so sorry.'

'I just hope he doesn't push for shared custody. It would mean the children might have to go to Australia for weeks at a time. I couldn't bear it.' She gave a strangled sob and covered her face. 'What am I to do?'

'When are you seeing him again?'

'Tonight.'

'At the dance? But what about Rob? It's your big night with him,' said Beth.

'Rob! The dance! I clean forgot. Grief, what a mess. I'll have to cancel.'

'Who? Zach or Rob?' said Beth.

'Do I hear my name being taken in vain?'

Amy gave a start and guilt washed through her. There stood a tall, burly man with sandy hair and brown eyes who was regarding her warmly.

'Rob!'

How long had he been standing there? Had he heard anything? Lord, things were getting worse by the minute.

'How's my favourite tea lady?' he said with a smile. 'Got a nice cuppa and plateful of food for your man? I'm in need of a little TLC after manning the bar for the past four hours.'

Amy cast a harried glance at Linda and Beth who were backing off to leave the two of them alone. She got to her feet and with jerky actions made him some tea and loaded some scones on a plate.

'Here you go.'

'Aren't you going to come and sit down with me? I haven't seen you all day. I've missed you.' He leaned over the servery and gave her a warm, lingering kiss on the lips. Amy was painfully aware that she felt nothing. She was numb from her encounter with Zach.

Rob's kiss hadn't ignited a single spark whereas Zach's brief touch had sent her blood sky-rocketing. Don't think about it, she silently admonished. Don't compare. It was not a good idea.

'I can't, Rob. I've already had my break. I'm needed here.'

'I'll come around the back, then.' He sat down in one of the chairs provided for the workers and bit into a scone. As he chewed, he cocked his head on one side. 'You OK, luv?'

Amy shrugged, battling a sudden thickening of her throat as a rush of tears threatened.

'No. I feel fine.'

'You don't look it. What's the problem?'

It was typical of Rob to notice when something was amiss. He was always so kind to everyone. It was one of the reasons Amy loved him. But this minute she could do without his solicitude. It could unhinge the fragile control she had on her precarious emotional state.

'I've had a bit of a shock.' Correction, a huge, life-changing one.

'What?' He took another bite of scone and licked strawberry jam off his upper lip.

'Zach has turned up.'

'Zach?'

'Zach Morgan. The children's father.'

'So? It was bound to happen sooner or later. Is that a problem?' he said calmly and then shot her a glance and realised it was. 'OK, I can see by your expression that it is. But hey, Amy, I don't get all uptight when my ex is about. It's not the end of the world. He probably just wants to see the kids. It's no big deal.'

'I don't want him around.'

'Sweetie, I don't think you have

much of a choice.' He drained his tea and put the empty cup and plate on the servery. 'Time for us workers to get back on the job,' he said, standing and pulling Amy close for a quick hug and kiss. She clung to him, willing his comforting strength to flow through to her and bolster her courage.

Rob nuzzled her neck and then said, 'I'll see you at the dance and then we can enjoy ourselves and celebrate.'

'I haven't said yes yet,' she pointed out, pulling away from his embrace, inexplicably miffed he was taking things for granted.

'But you will.' He kissed her again and left the marquee, his head held high, arms swinging, and radiating confidence.

Amy watched him go with a sinking heart. He was so sure of her but she had an awful premonition that his confidence was misplaced Suddenly she didn't think she could go through with it. Well, at least not at the moment. Not while there was unfinished business with Zach hanging over her head. And she certainly didn't feel like celebrating anything, engagement or not.

She wanted to go home and crawl under the duvet to lick her emotional wounds and hope the world would just go away and leave her in peace.

5

A pig on a spit had been roasting all day over an open fire. Delicious, mouth-watering aromas hung heavy on the humid, early evening air as the pork was carved up to feed those who were staying on after the fayre for the country dancing.

Amy had been looking forward to the dance, of celebrating her and Rob's engagement with friends. But not now. Zach's appearance had ruined all that.

Instead, Amy's head felt cleaved in two. Her neck and shoulders throbbed with tension. Her whole body was bruised and worn out with stress. She massaged her temples while listlessly watching the revellers on the grassy dance floor. At least she didn't have to worry about the twins. They were staying with her parents for the night so that, in theory, she and Rob could celebrate their engagement.

Hah, that was the theory. There was nothing to celebrate now. And if Zach continued to hang around, would there ever be? Her blind response to him earlier had given Amy a terrifying jolt.

It was if the last few years had never existed, as if time had rolled backwards and she was meeting Zach for the first time. The intense physical attraction between them was still very much in force.

At eighteen, she had gone to France to earn some money and enjoy a different culture before heading off to university. Zach had been working at the Blanchard family's vineyard to gain experience in wine making to benefit his own family's wine business back in Western Australia.

Zach had been a gorgeous string bean then, with a mop of unruly, jet-black hair, a sparse, athletic frame and a smooth boyish face hinting at the character of the man to come. It had been instant attraction on both sides.

The fires of passion had burned brightly for two halcyon weeks.

In hindsight, naivety and blind, trusting love had been Amy's undoing. She'd fallen for Zach Morgan hard and had presumed, by his sun-kissed words of love and tender actions, that the feeling was reciprocated. How foolish. She had given herself wholeheartedly. But it hadn't been enough. Chantelle Blanchard, with her classic beauty, sophistication and wealth, had won his heart.

And now Zach was back in her life, slicing open old wounds, making her revisit old, deep-seated hurts, and she didn't like it. Not one little bit.

She leaned her head on her hands and prayed that he would go away.

6

Zach studied the dancers flying around the makeshift dance floor. Where was Amy? It look him a while to locate her in the half-light of the summer evening. She was sitting on the grass, slightly apart from the crowd, hugging her knees.

The years had been kind to her. The soft, teenage curves had fined down, her face was now more angular, character more firmly etched on it. For all her prettiness at eighteen, she was now one very attractive woman. Zach felt a stir in his heart.

He itched to bury his fingers into the spun cloud of her golden hair, to discover if it was as silky as yesteryear.

Blast, but he knew nothing about those letters she claimed to have sent him. There had to be a perfectly logical explanation why he hadn't received them. He would find out. In the meantime, he refused to be put off by Amy. There was too much at stake.

'Not dancing, Amy?'

Amy started in surprise and scrambled to her feet, taking a defensive couple of steps backwards. She hadn't expected to see him tonight. She had rung and left a message with the Philpots, crying off from her appointment with him. She had felt both ridiculously relieved at getting a reprieve from his disturbing presence and disappointed.

'What are you doing here?' She wrapped her arms protectively around her body.

'I've come to see you.'

'But why?'

'I'm not here to make trouble. I just want to talk to you.'

Amy felt she was teetering on the edge of a black chasm. One false move and the stable balance of her life would be thrown into chaos. She had planned to move forward from being a single parent by marrying Rob and finally leading a normal family life, sharing the responsibility of raising children, and maybe having another baby.

Rob was offering her the chance to make it happen. Zach was threatening to destroy that chance. Why couldn't he back off, return to Chantelle, and quit messing up her own bid for marital happiness?

'I have nothing to say to you,' she said.

'But I have plenty I want to ask. I need answers. Details. There are years to catch up on. I want you to fill in the gaps about the children, about you.'

'No.'

Zach's face tightened, emphasising the hawkish cut of his features. 'Fine. We'll dance instead.'

'No!' He ignored her protest. He caught hold of her arm and pulled her into the melee. Amy dug in her heels, but Zach was too strong for her. She was buffeted on either side by exuberant dancers and dragged along by her determined partner. In the end, it was easier to give in than make a scene.

Zach kept her on the dance floor for ages, his hands warm and capable, holding hers and guiding their progress through the various dance sets.

Every dance was an agonising tango of emotion. And it was a crushing realisation that she'd never felt this alive in Rob's embrace.

At last Zach led Amy off the floor. Holding her hand in his, he took her to a secluded corner, away from the frenetic activity. Amy sank down gratefully on one of the many straw bales that had been scattered around for seats. Zach smiled down at her, flicking a finger over her hot, flushed cheeks.

'You look exhausted. I'll go and fetch us some drinks.' A few minutes later, he returned with a tall glass of lemonade for Amy and a beer for himself. He sat down next to her, stretching out his long, black denim-clad legs.

She took a hefty slug of her drink to hide her traitorous responses to his closeness. It was the wrong thing to do as Zach shifted his thigh a few millimetres nearer just at that moment. She inhaled sharply and the fizzy drink slid down the wrong way. Amy began to cough and splutter, gasping for breath, while her heart shuddered like a jackhammer.

'Potent stuff,' Zach laughed and thumped her on the back.

Potent? Yup, but it was Zach and not the lemonade that was potent. He was lethal! She struggled to compose herself and dragged the back of her hand over her watering eyes. Zach stilled the action, gently moving her hand away.

With his fingers firmly on her chin, he angled her face towards him and mopped her eyes with a large, white cotton handkerchief. The tender, intimate gesture was her undoing.

She swallowed nervously. No, she hadn't been imagining her reaction to him. Any breath left over from her coughing fit was immediately sucked from her lungs. Her chest tightened painfully and a rolling warmth began to unfurl deep within her.

Zach's fingers, at first hesitant, then gaining confidence, lingered on her smooth, translucent skin and trailed from one pale, coffee-coloured freckle to another in a slow, wondrous exploration. The caress was butterfly soft and delicate and caused Amy to shiver with every atom of her being.

Her lips parted on a sigh. Her eyes fluttered shut as she savoured the spiralling coil of desire that was unwinding from the depths of her being and sliding a deliciously slumberous heat through her veins.

It was madness to allow Zach to make her feel like this. Sweet madness. But, glory be, it felt good. Too good.

'Zach.' It was a mere whisper, as soft as a moth's wing.

'Hush.' He seemed to know what she wanted. His lips settled over hers, warm and melting and infinitely desirable.

Amy's eyes flew open and she reared

back, her hands straining against Zach's chest to force some kind, any kind, of distance between them.

Guilt fuelled her anger. 'Get your hands off me, Zach Morgan. Stop mauling me!' Self-loathing put a sting in her words. She shouldn't have let him kiss her. And she shouldn't have kissed him back!

'Hold it a minute, Amy Jones. You weren't exactly fighting me off just then. You were fully participating.'

Amy glared.

'Maybe. But I haven't forgotten about Chantelle. I'm not interested in affairs with married men. It's not my style. And for your information, Zach Morgan, even if you were as free as a bird, I still wouldn't want you.'

'Chantelle is no longer my wife,' he grated out. 'We're divorced. We didn't have kids. I'm single, unattached and perfectly within my rights to kiss another woman, especially one who happens to be my former lover and mother of my children.'

'Oh no, you're going to recognise paternity then?'

'Of course. Why wouldn't I? There's no denying they're my kids. You just have to look at them to realise that.'

'So? It doesn't mean you have to hang around. Can't you just go away again? We do fine without you. You're not needed.'

'You owe me some time with my children, Amy.' Ice cold fury was building within him. It crackled danger in every word. 'I wouldn't have left six years to find you if I'd known about the twins. I would have come immediately, regardless of my dad's health.'

'It's easy for you to say that now, but I really do have trouble accepting your ignorance over Luke and Emma. I only have your word for it. I needed you then.' I wanted you, she almost shouted. 'But you let me down, Zach Morgan, and I've learnt to live without you.'

'For Heaven's sake, Amy, stop being so antagonistic. Get used to the idea that I'm not going away until we're settled things between us. Is that so much to ask?'

'Yes!'

'Why?'

Where to start? How could she explain?

'Amy?'

She heard the appeal and sighed. 'What things have to be settled?'

Zach had the urge to say 'us', but he resisted. He would leave that touchy subject until a time when Amy was less hostile. 'The children, for starters,' he said.

'What about them?'

'They seem nice kids.'

'They are,' she arched up. 'Why wouldn't they be?'

'Relax. I'd like to get to know them better. I'd like to take them home to meet the folks and become acquainted with my country.'

'Australia?' Fear flowed through her veins. No! She didn't want them to go!

'I think they'd enjoy it. I know I'd

love to show them around. I want to make up for lost time.'

'No, I don't want them to go.'

'It'd only be for a few weeks.'

But what if he decided to keep them there? Amy read in the newspapers about fathers stealing their children. 'No!'

'Come on, Amy, don't be selfish. Aren't I entitled to some time with them? You've had them exclusively for five years. I've had one brief conversation with them.'

'No.'

'But you'll have a terrific time.'

He wanted her to go? No, absolutely not. The less time she spent with Zach Morgan the better. And anyway, Rob would hate her going off with an ex-lover to the other side of the world. It wouldn't be morally right.

Amy bit down on her lower lip and shook her head.

Zach reined in his frustration. He'd come on too strong, was trying to rush her. 'OK, Amy. You don't have to make a decision now.'

'We want nothing to do with you!' There was a desperate appeal in her voice, but Zach ignored it. He wouldn't give up. There was too much at stake.

'We'll let the twins have a say in that. Wouldn't you say that was fair?'

What did fairness have to do with it? Nothing! She felt completely trapped.

'I'll come around tomorrow to discuss it some more.'

Amy opened her mouth to make one more appeal. Zach placed his index finger over her lips to silence her. 'No, Amy. No more arguments. Until tomorrow.'

'There you are, luv.' It was Rob. He had two glasses and a bottle of champagne. 'I've been searching for you everywhere. Some of the gang said they saw you dancing with a tall, dark man. Sounds ominous,' he said jokingly.

Amy shivered. If only he knew how ominous.

'Now, I've got the champers and the

ring. All you have to do is say yes.' He glanced at her expectantly. There was dead silence. 'Amy?'

Her hands fluttered nervously and her bottom lip trembled. 'I'm sorry, Rob,' she whispered apologetically. 'I can't . . . '

'You're not turning me down?' His face was suddenly twisted in pain. 'You can't!' he said aghast. 'Not now.'

'I'm not making any decisions until I've wrapped up this business with Zach. It wouldn't be fair on any of us.'

'He's really got to you, hasn't he,' he said bitterly, sitting down heavily on the bale next to her and taking her hand in his. 'You shouldn't let him get under your skin.'

How could she be detached from Zach when all he had to do was look at her to make her insides melt? And his kiss had rattled her completely.

'When are you seeing him again?' said Rob.

'Tomorrow.'

'I'll try and be there too. You need

supporting. I won't let him bully you into anything you don't want to do.'

'You're too kind to me.'

'Why wouldn't I be? I love you. Now do you want to crack this champagne anyway?'

Amy shook her head. 'Save it.'

'OK, so let's dance instead.'

Amy didn't feel like dancing either, but at least while she was spinning around on the dance floor she didn't have to think or talk.

7

Sunday was dire, which was of no surprise to Amy. She hadn't expected anything less than awful.

She slept in late after a turbulent, troubled night and had eaten only a sketchy breakfast of tea and toast. Later, her mother, Fay, dropped the kids over and gave Amy a hard, significant look. Without saying a word, she picked up Amy's left hand and pointedly inspected her bare ring finger. Amy snatched her hand away.

'Are you going to tell me what happened yesterday? You don't give the impression of a blushing bride-to-be,' said Fay.

'No.' The last thing Amy wanted was to dissect the previous day's circus with her mum. Or with anyone, come to that. She was having a hard enough time working it all out for herself.

'I see.'

'No, you don't.' Amy sighed. She didn't want to hurt her mum's feelings, but at this moment she simply didn't want to discuss Zach Morgan in the vain hope that he might go away. 'Anyway, it's far too complicated to explain now, especially with the kids around.'

'It has nothing to do with Zach Morgan, I suppose?'

Trust her mum to have heard the gossip. Amy wasn't fooled by Fay's airy, unconcerned gaze. There was the light of investigative zeal in her eyes. She was eager to know everything. 'Not in front of the children, Mum,' she said repressively.

'Darling, they've been talking about nothing else all morning, as you'll soon discover. But if you want to play coy, we'll leave the subject until later. Far be it from me to force you to share things with your mother.'

After she had gone, Amy realised what Fay meant about the children.

They had lots to say on the subject of Zach. They went on and on about him, asking Amy endless questions. Amy tried very hard to be patient because she could understand their preoccupation. She, too, was more than a little preoccupied. But their continual badgering took its toll on her already fragile mental state.

She quivered with suppressed tension. She wasn't sure how she was going to deal with Zach, how to convince him that he was wasting his time, that they didn't want him around. Unfortunately, the way Emma and Luke were harping on Amy had a sinking feeling that she'd be battling them too.

Amy resorted to her usual stress therapy of cooking to help her maintain a modicum of sanity. The soothing mixing and beating of the creamy yellow batter did much to steady her nerves. Soon the kitchen was permeated with the hot smells of cinnamon buns and chocolate cake.

She was pulling a tray of melting moments out of the oven when the doorbell rang. She dropped the tray on the counter and swung around in a blast of nervous energy, her heart beating wildly.

He'd come.

The deep, burred voice rumbling in the hallway caused her to relax a fraction. It was Rob, and although she didn't really want to see him either, he was less of a threat than Zach. She forced her rigid lips into a smile. She didn't want Rob suspecting that she was less than pleased to see him. It wasn't his fault she was so keyed up. She returned to her biscuits, sliding them off the tray and on to a wire rack for cooling.

'Hello, luv,' he said as he strolled with easy confidence into the warm, aromatic kitchen. He kissed her cheek and then perched on one of the bar stools.

'Something smells good. Once we're married, I'll have to watch my weight.'

Amy didn't comment, but took

another tray of biscuits from the oven.

Rob sighed. His gaze swept around the kitchen. The implication of the cooking frenzy wasn't lost on him. He knew all about Amy Jones' cooking therapy.

'So has Morgan shown up yet?' Rob said, his voice carefully neutral.

Amy put down two mugs of coffee and sat down opposite him. She began to fiddle with the sugar bowl. 'No,' she said shortly. 'Not yet.'

'Relax, sweetheart. What can he do to you that's so terrible?'

Amy ground the spoon further into the sugar. 'He might want joint custody.'

'So?'

'I don't want the kids going to Australia.'

'He is their father, but it probably won't happen while they're so young. Don't worry about it.'

Amy concentrated on the sugar, digging the spoon in deeper and deeper.

'Any ideas why he's suddenly turned up,' pushed Rob.

'No. He claims he didn't know about the children until yesterday. He reckons he never got my letters.'

'You believe him?'

'Maybe. Yes, I suppose. He appears genuine though I can't believe he wouldn't have received my letters. I sent enough.'

Rob stared at Amy steadily. 'That means he came in search of you, not the kids. So what do you reckon of that?'

'I don't know! I hadn't even considered that aspect.' She'd been too busy panicking about her reaction to him and what he wanted with the children. Amy flung down the spoon, sending a shower of sugar granules over the scrubbed pine table. 'Once he's here we'll find out what he wants from us. From me.' Bitterness edged her words.

'He can't take anything that you're not willing to give.'

But that was the rub. How much was

she willing to give the man who had won her heart all those years ago? She hung her head so Rob wouldn't see the fear in her eyes that she would give Zach whatever he asked for.

'We can weather this storm, luv. You know we can. Just remember, I love you.'

Amy raised her head and stared into his kind, tea-brown eyes. Yes, she knew he loved her. He had been asking her to marry him for months now, but it had been her own doubts that had held her back from accepting him. She was deeply fond of him. But love? Was she selling them both short by agreeing to marry him?

Until yesterday, she believed they had as good a chance as anyone else from finding happiness in a comfortable, steady marriage.

Until yesterday, she had been sure of her needs.

Until yesterday, there hadn't been Zach.

Her eyes glistened with unshed tears.

'Yes, I know, Rob. Thank you.'

Rob's mobile phone rang. It was his ex-wife who needed him to collect their daughter, Teagan, from a friend's place.

'I'm really sorry, Amy, but I have to go.'

'Don't worry. I'll be fine. As you said, he can't hurt me. I'll cope just fine.'

She was a bundle of nervous energy and when she ran out of flour, she still couldn't give up on the cooking. It was the one thing keeping her calm. She rummaged about in her cupboards and then cast her eyes about for something, anything else to cook.

She zoomed in on the marrow that her mum had brought around this morning from her dad's vegetable garden. Hmm. She could make some chutney. That would keep her occupied.

Of course, the onions would make her cry, but she felt like crying anyway. They'd be a good excuse.

She sliced and chopped the marrow into a large saucepan and then started on the onions. She was sniffling over them when the doorbell rang. Emma materialised from wherever she'd gone to when Rob had arrived, and went to open the front door.

Her self-conscious giggles and the low pitch rumble of a man's voice alerted Amy that Zach was here. Amy sniffed and wiped her watering eyes as he sauntered into the kitchen.

He looked good. His thick black hair sprang untamed around his tanned, angular face. His hawkish features were softened by the good humour that played around his mouth and coal-dark eyes.

His expression was one of sensual, confidence. Faded blue jeans hugged his long, muscular legs, and a navy polo shirt was stretched enticingly across his wide, impressive chest.

But Amy wasn't fooled by his deceptive casualness. She could sense his watchfulness, his carefully leashed power. He carried with him a force field of suppressed energy. She could feel her own nerves crank up a notch.

She tried to ignore his impact on her.

Sniffing again, she carried on attacking her pile of onions. She derived a certain masochistic pleasure from the burning, pungent onion juice.

'So you finally bothered to turn up,' she said with unaccustomed tartness. It wasn't like her to be uncivil, but she couldn't help it.

'Missed me, sweetheart?' He flashed her a roguish grin. 'By the look of all this cooking, it was a good job I didn't come earlier. Appears you've been cooking up a storm.'

Amy didn't enlighten him that he was the cause of her cyclonic cooking jag. She didn't want him to know that he had her completely rattled. He had enough of an advantage as it was.

'Would you like some tea?' She plugged in the kettle before he could answer and filled a blue pottery plate with warm biscuits. Luckily, Emma chattered away to Zach non-stop because Amy couldn't think of a single thing to say. Her brain had turned to mush.

Luke came and joined them, bombarding Zach with corny jokes and questions, questions, questions. Neither child showed any signs of shyness.

Amy kept her head down and let the conversation ebb and flow around her. She was thankful that the twins always had plenty to say and Zach was an attentive listener, encouraging them to talk.

Amy chopped and sniffed, her nose turning cerise. She lent only half an ear to the chitchat until Emma said something significant. As the import of her words sunk in, Amy almost sliced her finger off.

'Can we go, Mum? Please?'

Amy whipped her finger into her mouth, wincing as the onion juice stung the fresh cut. She glared at Zach. 'I thought we were going to discuss it before involving the children?' she said around her bleeding finger.

She hoped she sounded calm and controlled, though inside she was livid. Zach had no right pre-empting things by asking the children outright. She wouldn't have a chance of dissuading them now.

'We are discussing it. As a family.' His smile was unrepentant, then his eyes narrowed in on her finger. 'Let's take a look at that cut.'

'No, it's fine.'

Zach ignored her. He scraped back his chair and came around to stand close to her. Too close. He gently eased her finger from her mouth and inspected the wound. Dark red blood, the colour of vintage claret, welled up from the small, deep cut.

'Do you kids know where the first aid stuff is?' he asked over his shoulder.

'Yes, upstairs in the bathroom cabinet,' said Emma.

'Right. Both of you go and get it, then, before your mother bleeds all over the floor.'

The children disappeared from the kitchen, leaving Amy and Zach alone.

Heat stung Amy's cheeks. She was transported back to the day she'd cut her finger while cutting grapes at the Blanchards' vineyard. The memory was indelibly etched on her heart. It had been the first time they'd kissed.

Amy snatched her hand away from Zach's disturbing clasp. She bolted over to the sink and ran the cold tap.

'Would you like me to put a Band-Aid on it?' His caressing voice shivered across her skin. He was right behind her, the noise of the gushing tap had masked his footsteps. The hairs on the back of her neck prickled with awareness. Her skin goose-bumped. Her breath caught mid-throat.

'No,' she squawked. 'I can manage.' She missed the glint of humour in Zach's dark grey eyes. She was as jumpy as a cat.

Interesting. It confirmed his opinion that she wasn't indifferent to him, whatever she claimed to the contrary. A smile tugged the corner of his mouth as he sat back in his chair and watched Amy struggling to get her emotions back under control while her shaking

74

fingers clumsily wound the tape around her finger.

Luke was hopping about the kitchen, waiting for his opening. He wasn't one to be sidetracked for long. While his mum fiddled by the sink, he said, 'So what about Australia, Mum? Can we go? Can we?'

Amy's gut reaction was a resounding, No! But the anticipation glowing in her children's faces made her waver. Zach was their dad, after all, and they were so thrilled to have met him at last. Could she be a killjoy and prevent them from spending time with Zach? No, not really. Not in all fairness.

But Amy had never felt less like being fair.

She took a deep breath. 'Maybe, but we've got to discuss it carefully. It's not easy just to pack your things and go.'

The children took this as a yes and cavorted around the kitchen in agonies of delight. Amy bowed her head over the sink and concentrated on washing up the debris from her cooking. Her eyes were so blurred she couldn't see what she was doing.

Sudsy water sloshed over the side and puddled at her feet. She barely noticed it. What had she started? Would there be any going back?

Salty tears fell and mingled with the bubbles.

8

'You're late,' the sour, sucking-lemons voice of Melanie Philpot accused Amy.

'Sorry.' Amy attempted to inject some sincerity into her apology. She failed. Noisily she continued stacking the breakfast dishes into the dishwasher while Melanie stood vibrating disapproval in the doorway.

Amy cursed her luck that she had to deal with Melanie rather than her mother on the one day of the year she'd overslept.

She'd woken late after a spectacularly bad night tossing and turning in bed. Nothing had been resolved from Zach's visit because the children had monopolised him for the whole afternoon and then he'd had to leave for dinner at the Philpots.

Amy had cooked everything possible in the house, had caught up with the ironing and then cleaned all of the downstairs to try and keep herself from going bananas thinking about Zach.

Rob had turned up later and they'd had their first major row, mainly over Zach and why she hadn't pushed him for answers as to why he was there.

Thank goodness Monday was her cleaning day at the Philpots. She didn't think she could have brazened it out if it had been her regular bookkeeping day at Rob's. She went cold at the mere thought. Life was becoming far too complicated.

'Once you've cleaned the kitchen and the dining room, the beds need to be stripped. I've left some delicates in my room that need careful handwashing. Oh, and you'll have to attend to the guest room too,' Melanie instructed.

'Right.' Amy crashed the pots and pans about in the sink, hoping Melanie would take the less subtle hint to leave so that Amy could nurse her troubled thoughts in peace.

No such luck.

'And we'll be wanting lunch on the terrace at one. Nothing too fancy. Cold meats, salads, cheese, grapes, French bread. The usual thing.'

Great. Not only was Amy way behind schedule, but she'd have to prepare a gourmet lunch too. And she wasn't fooled by Melanie's request for a simple meal. Thank goodness the local store had an upmarket delicatessen counter to pander to the likes of the Philpots.

She'd give them a quick ring and see what they could rustle up at short notice.

In Melanie's pink and peachy ruffled room, Amy ripped off the top sheet from the bed, rolling it into a loose ball before dumping it on the floor and attacking the pillow slips and bottom sheet. She gathered up all the bed linen in her arms, including the filmy wisps of satin and lace discarded by Melanie.

Throwing the sheets into the washing machine and leaving the handwashing for later, Amy set to work polishing and vacuuming the downstairs rooms.

The guest room was obviously Zach's. His jeans and blue shirt were lying over a richly-upholstered Queen Anne chair. Amy hesitated and then, her heart hammering and going against all her instincts of self preservation, touched them. Slowly she raised his shirt to her face and breathed in his scent.

She closed her eyes. Just the smell of him was enough to make her blood heat and her heart yearn. But it was foolish to tempt herself.

Resolutely she replaced the clothes. The bed was neatly made, clothes were hanging in the walnut wardrobe and an empty case was placed behind the chair. Amy flicked about with a duster and glanced at her watch. She was running out of time. She lingered for one long moment and then closed the door.

Back in the laundry room, she gave Melanie's delicates a quick whisk in some warm, soapy water and then took all the washing outside to peg on the line.

The air was heavy with the scent of Henry Philpot's roses and the lazy drone of bees. Amy felt her spirits lift for the first time that day. Things weren't too dire. Not really. Breathing in the rich pot pourri of honeysuckle, roses, stocks and pinks, Amy slung her first damp sheet over the line.

The kitchen garden was screened from the more formal part of the grounds by a rustic pine lattice that was covered with rambling roses of delicate shell pink. Melanie's precise cut-glass voice could be heard on the other side.

Amy swiped a worried glance at her watch. She mustn't be late for lunch and have Melanie on her back. Good. There was still half-an-hour to spare.

Amy finished hanging the linen and then started pegging up the lacy wisps. She flexed her shoulders and cracked a wary yawn as she bent over the wash basket. A second person spoke from the other side of the lattice. Amy's jaw snapped shut and she jack-knifed upright when she heard it.

81

Zach!

Amy's heart pumped hard, thudding against her ribcage like a mechanical battering ram. She tiptoed forward and craned her neck to try and glimpse him through the pink roses. She leaned further forward and a surge of unexpected emotion raged through her. Her blood began to boil. She was fired with inexplicable, red-hot jealousy.

He was walking arm in arm with Melanie across the precision-cut lawn, with his head attentively angled towards her. They looked very, very cosy and intimate.

Amy gibbered, ignoring the fact that it was none of her business what Zach did and with whom. He'd told her that he was a single man again and able to be with any woman he wanted. She was the one who wasn't free, but seeing him with Melanie hurt more than she could say.

She stomped back to the washing line and rammed the pegs on Melanie's washing, careless of damaging the fragile garments. She was furious with him and even more so at herself. His love life was nothing to do with her. She had to remember that.

Muttering curses under her breath, Amy failed to hear the couple's approach.

'These roses are spectacular.' Zach deep-timbred voice drifted through the lush, green screen of leaves. 'The whole garden is extremely beautiful. You must be very proud of it.'

'Yes,' Melanie replied with her habitual coolness. 'But one does become used to it. I quite take it for granted. Daddy, of course, likes to potter here after work, and Mummy cuts flowers to decorate the church once a month.'

'What's through there?'

'Oh nothing much. It's the gardener's domain. We don't need to go in there. It'll soon be time for lunch. Shall we go and freshen up?'

'I'd like to look around for a while longer, if that's all the same to you?'

'Fine, Zach. I'll leave you to your

little exploring and then see you on the terrace for an aperitif. Don't get lost.' She tapped him playfully on the arm. 'And don't be too long.'

'Amy!'

Amy froze, one hand holding a peg.

'What are you doing here?' Zach asked with pleased surprise. He hadn't expected to see her again so soon. He'd forgotten that she worked part-time for the Philpots.

'I could ask you the same question!' She thrust the peg on the dripping garment.

'Amy, what's up?'

'You seem on excellent terms with Melanie.'

'You're not jealous of Melanie, are you?' he murmured softly, closing the distance between them. He was pleased, not angry by her belligerence. If she was jealous, it meant she cared and that was a step in the right direction in his estimation.

'Of course not.'

'I can hardly ignore her while staying

here. She is Henry's daughter.'

'So why are you staying here?'

'I'm negotiating selling my family's wines through Henry's chain of liquor stores.'

'Oh. I see.' She felt foolish for overreacting. Amy took a step backwards and picked up the wash basket. She held it in front of her like a bulky shield. 'I've got work to do. I can't stand around talking to you all day. I've lunch to prepare.'

Amy ducked under the damp sheets and headed for the kitchen. But Zach was close behind.

'Why are you doing this sort of work? What happened to your plans to become a teacher?' he asked.

Amy reeled around to confront him. 'You have the nerve to ask me that?' she said with dangerous quiet. 'Have you forgotten that you got me pregnant? I was eighteen, Zach. I'd just started university. I thought I'd picked up a bug when I was so sick all the time and then I found out I was expecting the twins.'

Her fury mounted along with the rising tempo of her voice. 'Bang went all my plans for a degree and teacher training. How could I have possibly followed a career when I was a teenage single mother of twins? Get real, Morgan.'

Red slashed Zach's cheeks. 'I'm sorry, Amy. I suppose I haven't given that aspect much thought. I'm still coming to terms with being a dad. Give me time.'

Amy's anger abated slightly. 'Don't worry about it. I don't care about a career anymore. The children come first.'

Zach still felt driven to defend himself. 'Things may have worked out differently if you hadn't run out on me in France,' he challenged. 'If you'd stayed, we could have had a future together. Life could have been so different, Amy.'

'I very much doubt it. When I saw you kissing Chantelle, I was so shocked and hurt I could hardly think straight, and then later she told me that you two had been together for weeks. What did I have to gain from staying and listening to your lame excuses? No way was I going to hang around and be further humiliated.'

'Oh, come on, Amy. It was nothing like that! I didn't cheat on you. I was in love with you. Chantelle was never important.

'She was a friend and the daughter of my boss.'

'Just like Melanie Philpot. Can you see a pattern forming here? Anyway, Chantelle wasn't just a friend. I saw you kissing her.'

'Chantelle kissed me once. Once, Amy. There was no come on by me, I swear. Our relationship developed much later.'

'Oh, really!'

Zach dragged his hand through his hair in exasperation. He remembered the kiss because he'd been so surprised when Chantelle had launched herself into his arms and kissed him so soundly. He'd been too surprised to repel her. He wished he had, then he wouldn't be in this fix, trying to convince this perverse, beautiful woman that he'd only ever cared for her.

But she was determined not to be persuaded.

'Chantelle was attracted to me. It was her way of showing how she felt.'

'You expect me to believe that? You married her, for crying out loud. Are you going to tell me now that you didn't find her attractive too?'

'We didn't get married for two years,' Zach protested. 'We met again a year after I left France. She came out to our vineyard to gain experience, just as I had visited and worked on her father's property. We got on well, we had similar backgrounds, similar interests. It wasn't terribly surprising that we got married.'

'Are you telling me it was a marriage of convenience? I won't buy that, Zach. This is the twenty-first century.'

'I didn't say it was. Chantelle and I were fond of each other. It was no big

drama. The families thought it was an excellent idea. It cemented the tie between the two winemaking families. We thought it would work out. We're still good friends even though our marriage wasn't a huge success.'

'Why did you divorce?'

Zach shrugged. 'There was a spark missing, amongst other things,' he admitted with a touch of grimness remembering their bitter fights. He'd wanted children, Chantelle hadn't. 'But all that is irrelevant to us, Amy. It's the here and now I'm interested in. In us.'

'There is no us. Don't fool yourself to the contrary.'

'Of course there is! Get used to it.'

'You have no right to dictate to me, Zach Morgan.'

'Oh, here you are,' Melanie interrupted from the doorway. Her eyes slid from one rigid, angry face to the other. Amy acidly wondered how long Melanie had been standing there, listening to their heated exchange. Not that she particularly cared. She had gone beyond that point.

'Will lunch be much longer?' Melanie's reproach was loud and clear.

'No, it's almost done. Mr Morgan was about to join you.' She gave him a glacial glare. 'Weren't you, Mr Morgan?'

'Come along, Zach, Daddy has opened an excellent Verdelho that you simply must try.' Melanie linked her arm through Zach's and began to manoeuvre him out of the kitchen. Over her shoulder, she tossed dispassionately, 'Don't keep us waiting, Amy.'

Amy slammed the smoked salmon and cold meat on to platters. She haphazardly garnished with parsley and nasturtium flowers. She plonked some exotic cheeses on another plate and gave it the same treatment. It took her another ten minutes to finish preparing the salads and then she carried the food out to the terrace on a large tray.

She clenched her jaw as she approached the chattering, laughing group and banged the tray down on the wrought iron,

Mediterranean tile table. She refused to meet Zach's eyes, though she could feel his gaze boring into her.

'That will be all for the time being.' Melanie dismissed her in clipped accents.

Back in the kitchen, Amy tidied up and then prepared the fruit and cheese platters, along with the coffee, and took it along to the terrace.

Mellowed by the tasty food and excellent wine, Henry Philpot was feeling expansive. 'Delightful meal, Amy, m'dear. No wonder Thurley wants to snap you up. If I were twenty years younger I wouldn't mind having a bash at courting you m'self. Haw, haw!'

He was oblivious to the sudden, stony silence of his business colleague.

'Who's Thurley?' Zach asked with lethal calmness. He pierced Amy with interrogating black eyes. She spun around so she didn't have to face him and hurriedly, clumsily stacked the dirty dishes. 'Amy?'

'Oh, Thurley's a good fellow,' Henry

Philpot carried on, heedless to the turbulent undercurrents swirling around him. 'He runs the builders' yard in the village. Thurley and Amy have been an item for years. Isn't that right, m'dear?'

'Sort of. For a few months at any rate.' Scarlet-faced, Amy heaved up the laden tray. She cast a nervous glance towards Zach. Thunderclouds darkened his beautiful face. His thick, black brows had snapped together to form a forbidding straight line. Uh-oh, perhaps she'd made a tactical mistake not telling him about Rob.

'You're getting married soon, aren't you, Amy?' Sugar-coated acid dripped off Melanie's tongue.

'Nothing's settled.' Amy could see the fury mounting by the second in Zach's hard, slate-grey eyes.

'Rob was telling me that he hoped for an autumn wedding. Not too long to wait then, m'dear,' said Henry.

Zach uncoiled his powerful frame from the iron chair and raised himself to his full, impressive height. With menacing deliberation, he covered the distance between himself and Amy in a couple of strides.

Amy took a defensive shuffle backwards, hampered by the heavy tray. With deadly care, Zach detached the tray from her nerveless fingers and set it back on the tiled table. He then took a firm grip of Amy's shaking shoulders, his arctic stare boring hard into her. 'Is it true? Are you going to marry this Thurley bloke?'

Amy tried to wiggle out of his grasp, but his fingers only bit deeper into her flesh. 'Answer me, for goodness sake!'

Henry Philpot spluttered a protest, but Zach ignored him. His eyes were riveted on Amy's.

'Of course she's marrying Rob Thurley,' Melanie said with a tinkling laugh. 'Everyone in the village knows that. It's common knowledge. I don't know why you're acting so coy, Amy.'

Amy stood frozen to the spot. What could she say? Zach's fingers dug deeper. She winced at the pressure and raised trembling hands to tug at his wrists, trying to break the contact. 'You're hurting me.'

'Is it true?' His voice was hoarse. With pain? Ridiculous!

Her mouth opened and shut a couple of times. No sound came out. She cleared her throat and tried again. 'Yes.' It was barely a whisper.

Zach swore. His eyes glittered with a dangerous icy fire. 'I don't believe you. Tell me you're lying!' He thrust his face millimetres from hers. Amy recoiled at the bitter fury she'd unleashed.

'It's true. I'm marrying Rob.'

'Why didn't you say something before? Didn't you think I had a right to know?'

'I didn't think it was relevant. I thought you'd be leaving again soon, going back to Australia and I'd never see you again.'

Zach ran his hand through his hair and then his eyes lighted on her hand. 'You're not wearing his ring,' he said triumphantly, snatching up her left hand.

'We haven't chosen one yet,' she lied, knowing that Rob had had one picked out for weeks, but not wanting to rub salt into the wound.

Zach released her hand in disgust. Amy clasped it to her chest, holding it tight against her rapidly drumming heart, wondering what he was going to do next. The angry rigidity of his face was alarming.

'I don't believe this. You can't marry him!'

'You can't stop me.'

Amy snatched up the loaded tray and all but ran to the relative safety of the kitchen, hoping he wouldn't follow, but if he did she would stand her ground. If she wanted to marry Rob, that was her affair, not Zach's. He would be returning to Australia soon anyway. She still had her own life to lead once he'd gone.

It sounded good in theory.

She was relieved when Zach didn't come after her and she didn't have to put her bravery to the test.

9

Amy quickly dragged a brush through her tangled golden curls. Zach had just arrived at her cottage. The children had let him in, as she'd been upstairs tidying up, and they had called her to come and see him. But what did he want? To hassle her about Rob? She hoped not.

She slicked on a coat of dusky pink lipstick and rubbed a smidgen of blusher over her pale cheeks. She frowned at her reflection. Nah, too much.

She grabbed a tissue and ruthlessly scrubbed off the lippy and blusher. Now her lips looked full and swollen. As if she'd been kissed. And her cheeks glowed from the friction. As if she'd been kissed. Couldn't be helped. He wouldn't notice anyway. He was probably still spitting mad at her.

Amy glanced down at her old faded jeans and pink T-shirt that she'd been wearing all day. She'd better change. No, she wouldn't, she wasn't going to any fuss just to see Zach. And she didn't want him thinking she was dressing up for his benefit.

She slipped down the stairs and stood, unseen, in the kitchen doorway. Zach was sitting at the table laughing and chatting with the children. There was no sign of his earlier anger. He appeared relaxed and full of good humour. Amy steeled herself to go in, but was pre-empted by Emma.

'Hey, Mummy, Dad's telling us all about his home in Australia.'

Dad? How long had they been calling him Dad? Amy's stomach double knotted with tension. She hazarded a nervous, polite smile in his direction.

He didn't smile back, but subjected her to a hard, assessing once over. She hoped he wouldn't notice the bruised smudges under her eyes, the results of her sleepless night and then compounded by her crying jag when she'd returned from the Philpots.

'We've been talking about going to Australia,' Luke informed his mother with an enthusiasm that made her wince. 'Could we go in the summer holidays, Mum?'

'I need to discuss it with your father.' She stumbled over the last word. It sounded strange saying it after all these years.

'What's there to discuss? I'm more than happy with that arrangement. The sooner the better as far as I'm concerned.'

'Yes, well, I'm afraid it's not that straightforward.'

'Why?'

'I need to see if Mum or Dad are free.'

'Why?' Zach frowned. Was he missing something here? Why did her parents have to come? He didn't mind, but . . .

'I can't let the kids go off on their own. They're only five.'

'Yes, Amy, I appreciate that. It goes

without saying. But you and I will be there too. surely that's perfectly adequate, even by your standards?'

'I'm not going.'

There was a jarred silence. 'But Mummy, you have to come,' said Emma.

'I can't darling. I have work commitments and Rob might not like me going.'

'Why wouldn't Rob like it?' said Luke innocently.

Amy awkwardly wriggled in her chair. 'Because he wouldn't.'

The children turned puzzled faces to first Amy then Zach.

He regarded them thoughtfully. 'Shall I tell them why or will you? As it's obvious that, like me, they are totally in the dark about your relationship with this Thurley.'

'Tell us what?'

Amy glared at Zach. 'Just go ahead and discuss my private business with everyone!'

'Luke and Emma are hardly everyone. And neither am I come to that.

Don't you think your immediate family should be told that you're going to be married in a few weeks time?'

'Mum?'

Amy ignored Luke's plea for clarity and reassurance. She was too hung up on Zach's words. 'You,' she stabbed a finger towards him, 'are not immediate family.'

'Sorry to disabuse you, my sweet, but I am. I'm the father of Emma and Luke. That's pretty immediate by my reckoning. And if you think I'm going to sit back and allow you to bring a step-father, a complete stranger, into their lives without so much as a by-your-leave, then you've got rocks in your head, woman.'

'Rob is not a stranger. The kids have known him for years.'

'But I haven't, and I thought you said you'd only been going out with him for a few months? Or were you lying?'

'No! He's been a friend for years. We went to school together, for goodness sake, but we've only been dating for a few months.'

'Mum?' Luke interrupted them. 'You're not going to marry Rob, are you?'

'Please don't, Mummy. I don't want a step-dad. We've got our proper daddy now,' added Emma.

Zach's lips tilted into a humourless smile, a gleam of triumph in his eyes.

'But your father lives in Australia. He won't be around all the time,' Amy ground out, furious with the children and Zach for ganging up against her. 'And as far as Rob is concerned, there's nothing wrong with him. He's a lovely guy. You both get on well with him. You like him.'

'Yes, but that doesn't mean we want you to marry him,' said Emma with a pout.

'Why not? Aren't you pleased that Rob makes me feel special?' Amy experienced a fierce satisfaction as Zach's triumphant smile was wiped from his face.

Emma's dark grey eyes, so like Zach's filled with tears, contrite, Amy hugged her daughter and smiled reassuringly at her scowling son. 'Anyway, I won't be marrying Rob for ages, so there's no need to make a fuss about it. It's far too early days to be making plans.' Her voice was soothing and confident. 'We'll talk about it all later when we're on our own,' she added pointedly.

There was a perfunctory knock on the back door and, right on cue, Rob strolled in. He hadn't stood on ceremony for months, always assured of his welcome, but today was different. He realised it as soon as he stepped over the threshold and four pairs of eyes swivelled towards him.

Amy's were bright with tears, the twins had identical accusatory expressions, and the way Zach was regarding him, Rob reckoned he was lucky to have any hide left by the scorching disdain emanating from them.

Rob's confident grin slipped. 'Am I

interrupting anything? Shall I call back later?'

'No, no!' Amy quickly reassured him, though silently wishing him in the back blocks of Siberia. She released Emma and moved towards Rob for their customary kiss of greeting. Before she could reach him, Zach firmly moved her to one side and held out his hand to Rob.

'I hear congratulations are in order, Thurley.' There was no warmth in the greeting.

'Oh, really. Yes, of course.' Rob was thrown off balance. Embarrassed, he glanced at Amy. Why was Zach Morgan, congratulating him? Had Amy told him they were getting married? If that was the case, she could have at least told him first.

'But don't for one minute think that it's over, that you've won her,' Zach continued with icy menace. He snatched up Amy's left hand and held it aloft. 'You haven't got a ring on her finger yet. And while there's any breath in my body, I'll see to it that you won't! She's mine. Always was. Always will be.'

He released her hand, but grabbed her shoulders and delivered a swift, bruising salute on Amy's shocked, slightly parted lips. 'She's mine!' He kissed her again and then abruptly let go of her and stalked out of the house without so much as a backward glance.

The twins shot out after him. The door slammed. A ghastly, pressing silence descended on them, broken only by the steady tick, tick, tick of the kitchen clock on the mantel above the fireplace.

Tentatively, Amy raised her shaking fingers to her lips. She was appalled at Zach's sudden possessive behaviour. Who did he think he was, treating her as his chattel, branding her with his kisses, threatening Rob? She quickly dropped her hand to her side as she realised Rob was staring at her, a question in his eyes. She shrugged helplessly.

'I'm sorry.' It sounded totally inadequate. 'I don't know what got into him.'

'Why was he congratulating me? And threatening me? What's going on, Amy?'

Amy's knees were trembling. In fact, her whole body was shivering like an aspen leaf. She sank down into a chair and buried her head in her hands. 'You don't want to know.'

'Actually, I do, Amy. I don't like the way he was treating you. I presume you've told him you're going to marry me, and yet you've not said anything to me. So, I repeat, what's going on? I think I have a right to know.'

Amy squeezed her eyes tight shut. She couldn't do it, couldn't say it. At least not today, not while she could feel the warm imprint of Zach's lips on hers. It would be wrong.

This was all so crazy. A week ago she'd been set to marry Rob. She'd had no doubts. Now she was riddled with them. The trouble was she'd tasted heaven again and was worried that anything else would pall into insignificance. What was she going to do?

'Are you going to marry me, Amy?' he demanded when she didn't answer.

Was she? He was kind and stable and would be a good provider. But those insidious doubts kept nibbling away at her resolve.

The reasons that had been so acceptable a week ago now sounded inadequate and pitifully shallow. Amy was wretched. Everything was going awry. She didn't want to hurt Rob. He'd been so good to her. So kind and loving and understanding, waiting for her to feel comfortable in their relationship, never forcing her to go further than she wanted.

But Heaven forgive her, she wanted Zach!

Though she hated his arrogance, his insistence they belonged together, that she was his, deep down there was the suspicion that he was right.

He'd thrust himself back into her life

and turned it completely around. Her feelings for Rob couldn't compete. They were water to Zach's blood, air to Zach's fire. But was she brave enough to embrace a relationship with Zach again?

She didn't want to get hurt a second time.

Rob offered the safer life, the more comfortable existence.

But was that fair on Rob? She would have to tell him one way or the other if she was going to marry him.

And soon.

But not today.

No, not today. She needed time to sort herself out and be one hundred percent sure about what she really wanted from life.

10

It was hot. The sun bounced off the white concrete yard, radiating a harsh, unforgiving glare. Rob and a couple of other men were loading sacks of cement on to a lorry. Their checked shirts stuck wetly to their broad backs. Sweat rolled down their red faces.

They cussed good naturedly about the sweltering heat and how any self respecting man would be down the pub with a pint in front of him on such a day. As they laughed, a sleek, black Jaguar purred into the builder's yard and came to a halt under the only bit of shade in the whole place. They paid it scant attention.

Zach, cool and lean in a tailored charcoal suit, stepped out of the Jaguar and locked it with the remote control. He strode purposefully towards the building supplies shop, barely acknowledging the others.

'Can I help you?' called out Rob. 'Oh, it's you.' The temperature plummeted by several degrees.

'Thurley.' Zach executed a curt, dismissive nod and kept walking towards the square redbrick building.

'What do you want?'

'Nothing that concerns you, mate. I'm here to see Amy.'

Rob pokered up, his body taking on a bulldog stance. 'You leave her alone!' Zach ignored him. He was already half way across the forecourt. 'Hey!'

Zach halted and looked back over his shoulder. 'You planning on stopping me?'

'Now see here — !' Anger mottled Rob's already heat flushed face.

'Don't be ridiculous, Thurley. What do you think I'm going to do to her?'

Rob's face deepened to almost purple. 'She doesn't need you here messing up her life.'

'I have no intention of causing Amy problems.' Zach retraced his steps until he was barely a foot from Rob. He topped him by a good six inches. 'But I suggest you back off while Amy and I deal with our unresolved issues. You're the one causing her the extra stress by hanging about. You'd do her a great favour by making yourself scarce. She has a lot to contend with at the moment and it doesn't help having you around hassling her.'

Rob bristled, his chin jutting out. 'I'm the one she leans on. I'm the one who gives her the emotional support she needs.'

'Not any more, mate. You're redundant. From now on, it's me she'll be relying on.'

'You can't come and force yourself upon us!' But he blustered into thin air. Zach was off, marching across the concrete yard, and disappearing through the shop door. Rob ran after him, catching Zach just as he reached the office door. 'Did you hear me?'

Zach spun around. 'Lay off,' he said.

'This is my outfit. You've no right being here.'

'I want nothing from you, Thurley, but I have every right to see Amy.'

'What rights, for goodness sake?'

'For starters, she's the mother of my children.'

'What, the kids you've only just decided to recognise after five years of silence? What sort of father does that make you? And what sort of man to leave Amy alone and pregnant at eighteen?'

He'd hit a nerve. Silver fury burned in Zach's flint eyes. 'It's none of your damn business, Thurley. I'm here now to make amends for those lost years and I'm more than willing to shoulder my responsibilities.'

'You keep away from her.'

'Make me.'

'Rob?' Amy said. Their argument had brought her out from the back storeroom where she had been stocktaking. She held a sheaf of paperwork in her hands and had a pencil stuck behind her ear. She looked fresh and trim in a mint green, sleeveless dress and tan sandals.

Her cheeks turned a delicate meringue pink as she realised it was Zach causing the commotion with Rob. 'Zach!'

'Morning, sweetheart.' Zach planted a kiss on her sweet, rosebud mouth. Amy was too stunned to duck it. The pink turned to crimson.

'Zach!'

'Don't worry, luv. I'll throw him out.'

Amy switched her attention to Rob. He'd squared up in the doorway and was spoiling for a fight. His fists were clenched and his jaw was thrust forward. At school he'd earned a bad reputation as a scrapper. Amy thought he'd left all that behind, but obviously not.

The last thing she wanted or needed was for these two men to get into a brawl. She flashed a glance back to Zach. He stood with arrogant nonchalance, hands buried into the pockets of his superbly-tailored trousers, his black, fathomless eyes fixed on something far away. He looked cool and detached . . . and intimidating.

But Amy wasn't fooled by his casual stance. A nerve twitched in his cheek and there was an air of coiled menace kept firmly leashed. She had no doubt that he'd handle himself ably in any fight.

Rob might be all muscle from his tough, manual work of hauling bags of cement and lengths of timber about, but Zach had a body of pure, high tensile steel.

'It's OK, Rob.' Quickly she tried to defuse the situation. 'I can handle this.'

'But, Amy.'

'Really. I'll be fine.'

'But . . . '

'You heard the lady. Beat it.'

'All right, Zach, you don't have to interfere.' Amy frowned at him.

He grinned back, totally unrepentant. Rob took a step forward, knuckles raised.

'Rob!' It was now Rob's turn to earn a frown. She threw up her hands in

113

despair. 'For goodness' sake, the two of you. Quit being so juvenile. Rob, you'd better go back to loading Stan's truck or you'll have a riot on your hands. He's already behind on his contract and he won't take kindly if you delay him some more.'

11

She marched over and pushed Rob back out of the door. Instead of leaving, he made a grab for her and kissed her hard and long on the mouth.

Amy suffered it, more through embarrassment than anything else. Rob had never kissed her at work before. It's unexpectedness almost made her recoil. He smelt and tasted of sour sweat and anger. So different from Zach's cool, firm salute which had whipped all the oxygen from her bloodstream, in spite of its brevity.

She shut her eyes and let Rob have his moment of triumph, because that was what it was all about. Rob besting Zach. She was a pawn in their stupid macho game. Right on cue, Amy heard a harsh intake of breath from Zach.

Rob closed the kiss and smiled a superior smile. His hazel eyes gleaming with satisfaction. Obviously he hadn't noted her lack of response. He'd been too busy scoring points off Zach. Amy inwardly sighed.

'When you've quite finished, Thurley.' Zach's ice-cold voice sliced through the thick, charged air.

Rob immediately bunched up at the veiled threat. His eyes fixed challengingly on Zach. He lent forward to reclaim Amy's mouth. She saw it coming this time and ducked.

She didn't want to be party to their ridiculous one-up-manship. They were like a couple of stags.

'For heaven's sake, Rob, go! You're needed outside. And you, Zach, make it snappy. I've a pile of work to do. It's stocktaking time.'

She pushed past Zach to go into her small, functional office with its wall-to-wall grey filing cabinets and black steel desk. The one small window was open as wide as possible to let in the sultry summer air. Through the window drifted sounds of the men in the loading bay. Farther off, a dog barked.

Amy dropped her papers on the desk, conscious that Zach was lounging against the doorjamb, his long, lean length too disturbingly close for comfort. It was only a small office and he was a big man with a giant force field of sensual energy and it was all directed at her.

'So how do you feel when he kisses you, Amy?' Zach asked with deceptive softness. 'Do you melt like you do with me? I must admit, I didn't feel any rise in temperature. In fact, you didn't seem to be enjoying yourself very much at all. Were you?'

Amy blushed. She was glad she had her back to him. 'None of your business. Why are you here? What do you want?' She was pleased her voice sounded crisp and impersonal. Inside she was raging.

'To ditch Thurley for a start.'

'Get real.'

'It's cruel to string him along, especially as you can't possibly marry him now.'

'Why not? Nothing has changed.' She lied. With Zach back in her life, everything had. But would she admit that to him? No way!

'It's your turn to get real, my sweet. As I'm now here, back in your life, Thurley is surplus to requirements. You can put that in your stocktaking report, if you like.'

Amy rolled her eyes and refused to comment.

'Don't you think Thurley would appreciate such a memo? Maybe not, but his time is up and the sooner he knows it the better for all of us.'

'I don't see it that way. If anything, you're the one who isn't required around here.'

'Dear heart, I'm not leaving.'

So he kept telling her. Honestly, he'd caused her more heartburn these last four days than she'd suffered during the whole of the twins' pregnancy, and that was saying something. 'And? You being here doesn't mean that you can start dictating my every move, Zach Morgan.

118

If I want to marry Rob, I shall and neither you nor anyone else will be able to stop me.'

'Ah, 'if'. That's very telling.'

'When, if. It's all semantics.' Amy shuffled her papers and began to sort them into piles of no particular order. She wanted to appear busy and efficient, even though her mind was spinning out of orbit.

'You don't love him, you know.'

'So now you're a mind reader and heart psychologist. What a versatile, clever man you are.'

'I believe you're a one-man woman, Amy Jones. My woman.'

A stack of invoices fell to the floor. He made her nervous. 'Please, Zach. This is getting us absolutely nowhere. State your business and then go away so I can get on with my work. I have so much to do and I've got to be home for the twins at three.'

Zach sauntered farther into the confined office and hitched his hip on the side of her desk. He picked up a pen and absently fiddled with it between his long fingers while studying Amy. She looked terrific in green. It brought out the colour of her expressive eyes that were now regarding him with a great deal of wariness. He sighed and tossed the pen down.

'I've come to say goodbye.'

12

Amy gasped. Her stomach hit rock bottom. Acute disappointment washed through her. He was leaving? Now? When would she ever see him again? The thought was chilling. How could she ever survive without seeing him?

'I have to go to France today. I'll be gone for a week.'

Intense relief flooded Amy's entire being. He was only going for a week. Hallelujah. He wasn't leaving at all. She felt seriously light-headed.

And it also gave her a week's respite. A week to regroup her defences. Her mind skidded to a halt as Zach's cool fingers suddenly closed around her hand.

'There's no need to look so pleased about it,' irony edged his words. 'I've had this trip to the Blanchards organised for a long time. If I hadn't, I wouldn't be going. I'd much rather stay with you, but I can't disappoint them.'

'So you're going to see Chantelle?' Jealousy instantly spiked her heart.

'Of course.'

She wished she hadn't asked. She didn't want to know. Chantelle was the last person she wanted Zach seeing. She still couldn't forgive the French woman for her underhanded dealings with Zach six years ago. She still didn't trust her.

'How civilised.' She tried to extricate her hand from Zach's grasp, now mad at him. He could leave and good riddance.

'At her wedding.'

Her hand stilled. 'Oh.' Perhaps she could be magnanimous where his ex-wife was concerned after all.

Zach smiled. He'd noted the flare of jealousy in those beautiful green eyes at the mention of Chantelle. 'She's marrying a French fellow who's also in the wine business.'

'Another business merger. How nice.'

'Come with me.'

There was a heart's beat pause as Amy surprised herself by actually considering accepting his invitation. Then commonsense reasserted itself. 'No.'

'It'd be a good opportunity to spend some time together.'

'I don't need any time with you.'

'Amy, a hundred years wouldn't be long enough. All I'm asking is for a lousy week. We have so many things to discuss.'

'I have already agreed that you can have the twins for four weeks. What more do you want?'

'A whole lot more, but unfortunately there's no time to discuss it now. I've a meeting with Henry Philpot's directors and then I'm off. You have three hours to change your mind and come with me.'

'I shan't.'

Zach looked at her levelly and then stood. 'I see. At least say goodbye to the kids for me. Tell them I'll bring them back something.'

'You mustn't spoil them.'

'I've no intention of doing so. One small present isn't going to change their universe. And anyway, I've five years of present-giving on which to catch up.' He leaned over and picked up her hand, raising it to his lips and kissing it palm upwards.

He curled her fingers over the moist, tingling skin and replaced her hand on the desk. 'I'll see you when I return.'

Amy sniffed at his arrogance. 'Stay away two weeks, six months, a year, an eternity. It's all the same to me.'

'You are such a terrible liar.' He grinned at her from the doorway and then was gone.

She stared at the empty space for a full thirty seconds and sighed. Slowly she unclenched her fingers. Her palm looked normal. But he had branded her. Again. Every time he touched her or kissed her, he left his invisible mark.

She slowly raised her palm to her

own lips and held it there for another few seconds.

She dropped her hand and sighed again. Dejectedly, she regarded the mess on her desk. She really did have her work cut out now, sorting all the piles of papers back into their correct order. She glanced at the empty doorway. Of course, she could go to France instead . . . It was very tempting.

But she had Emma and Luke to consider.

And Rob.

What was she going to do about him? He was pressurising her to say yes and set a date, but the more he pushed the less she wanted to commit.

She had to decide what to do. Maybe with Zach away for the week she'd be able to make a decision. One way or the other.

13

'Mummy, can I wear lipstick? Teagan does and she's only a little bit older than me,' said Emma. 'Her mum says it's OK.'

Teagan was in the same class as the twins and she did a lot of things that Amy didn't approve of. She was a saucy minx. She was also Rob's daughter, her prospective step-daughter.

'No lipstick. No argument. Luke, brush your hair.'

'I have.'

'What with? Your toothbrush! Not good enough. Go and do it again, properly this time. And hurry, or we'll be late.'

'I feel sick.'

'It's just nerves, Em. Breathe deeply, but do it as you go. We're running out of time.' Amy hustled them outside.

It was the end-of-year school concert

and both children had solo parts. It wouldn't do to be late or their ferocious spinster headmistress would reduce the three of them to quivering wrecks.

'Will Dad be there?' Luke asked.

'He said he would.' Amy had received a phone call from Zach a few hours before saying that he was due to catch the ferry and would be there in plenty of time.

He'd sounded warm and friendly, but Amy was mad at him. She'd heard things on the village grapevine. 'Isn't Melanie with you?' she had blurted out.

She hadn't meant to say anything, but she'd been fuming ever since Mrs Bennett from the local shop had told her that Zach and Melanie had gone to France together. As a couple, the old lady had said with disapprovingly raised eyebrows.

Zach had gone so quiet on the phone that Amy had wondered if she'd been cut off.

'Yes,' Zach had suddenly broken the short, stark silence.

'Is she right next to you?' she'd asked suspiciously.

'Yes. I can't talk now. We'll discuss things later.'

Amy had flung down the telephone and steamed off to the kitchen. Later! She didn't want to see or talk to him later. Just thinking of him with Melanie made her blood boil. She dragged out her mixing bowl from the cupboard, slammed down spoons and knives, threw ingredients haphazardly on to the table and then stood staring at it helplessly.

Her mind was blank, there was a red-hot pressure behind her eyes, but the tears wouldn't come. They just kept building up and up and up like an impending storm on a muggy, summer's day.

'I hate him.' She cracked an egg into the bowl. 'Hate him.' She broke another. 'Hate him.' The eggs slipped around in the bottom of the bowl. She picked up the whisk and beat them with a wealth of frustration. They frothed in double quick time.

She stopped, her wrist aching. 'So why do I feel so wretched that he's with another woman? It doesn't make sense.'

If she married Rob she wouldn't ever have to worry about him being unfaithful. He was as straight as a die. But did she want to marry Rob, for all his good points?

No.

Though she hated to admit it, no had to be her answer.

He was pushing for her decision, but he wouldn't like it. Regardless of how things panned out with Zach, the last few days had made her realise that she didn't love Rob deeply enough to marry him. He was good, he was kind, he was steady, but she wanted more and wasn't prepared to compromise both of them by settling for second best.

All she had to do now was tell him, which was easy to say, but hard to do. Amy was dreading it.

★ ★ ★

It was hot and stuffy in the school hall even though the windows were wide open to allow in as much cool air as possible. But it was as muggy outside as it was in. A storm was brewing.

The flying ants were about, along with the midges. Chairs scraped back and forth, there was the babble of excited conversation and a fractious baby was taken outside to yell its head off. Rob's shoulder brushed Amy's as he sat down next to her.

'Hi, luv,' he said. She managed a strained smile. Luckily, Rob's attention was monopolised by his neighbour who was building an extension and wanted some advice. Amy gazed around the hall, slightly more relaxed now that they were here and the twins were backstage, but still keyed up with the knowledge that she had to talk to Rob.

She was also tense with the prospect of seeing Zach.

She waved to a couple of her friends and then smiled at a woman whose child was in the twins' class. In the next instant her smile froze. Her heart gave a jolt and started careering at full pelt.

Zach was already here. He was standing by the hall entrance. He radiated supreme confidence and power. His tall, athletic frame was clothed in the same charcoal grey suit he'd been wearing when she'd last seen him.

His black hair was slicked back from his face, accentuating his strong cheekbones and wide forehead, but for all his sophistication, he had the air of a ruthless pirate. All he needed was a cutlass and kerchief. Piercing jet black eyes scanned the packed auditorium. He was searching. For the twins? For her?

Amy slunk down in her seat as low as she could go. She wasn't quite ready to meet him yet. Her nerves were shot. She felt like a teenager suffering from a huge crush. She hiked up the concert programme to shield her face and prayed that she would blend into the crowd.

No such luck.

It was uncanny. He must have had an inner radar system especially tuned into her because the next instant he was making his way along their row. He excused himself with easy charm as he brushed against people's knees and bags until he was near to Amy and planted himself in the empty chair beside her.

'Hello, sweetheart.' He picked up her hand and turned it over, palm up. Goodness, he was going to kiss it. Quickly she pulled back. The momentum brought Zach forward and, instead of kissing her hand, he kissed her mouth. Hard. Swift. Intoxicating.

He eased back, lips curved into a smile, black eyes twinkling satisfaction. He tucked her hand into the crook of his arm and settled himself comfortably.

'Zach!' Now her heart was seriously racing. If it went any faster it would break out of her chest and gallop away out of the hall.

'Ssh. They're about to start.'

The lights dimmed. The drums rolled. Amy's heart kept fast time.

Rob, unaware of Zach's arrival, claimed Amy's other hand. Embarrassment coursed through her. She couldn't sit here at the school play holding hands with two men. It just wasn't on. She tugged first at one hand, then the other. Neither man took the hint. She was stuck.

'Relax, honey,' Zach whispered close to her ear. Too close. His warm breath caressed her skin and sent her goosebumps bumping. She could smell his particular spiciness.

It conjured up sunshine and sea and the sharp tang of eucalyptus leaves. Rob often smelt of brickdust and plaster. She knew which she preferred.

She tugged again. 'Let go,' she hissed at Zach. 'I've got an itch.'

14

The curtains whooshed open and the show began. After a while, Amy managed to extricate her hand from Rob's relaxed clasp, but Zach wasn't so easy to shake off. Every so often, Amy gave an experimental tug.

He just tugged back, drawing her closer each time. So she gave up and tried to ignore the way his fingers snugly entwined with hers.

The twins were great. They didn't forget their lines and their exuberance shone through. When Emma did an unsteady little curtsey at the end of her performance, Zach squeezed Amy's hand tight and shot her a proud glance. 'Cute,' he'd said. 'Very cute.'

She grinned and detected the glisten of moisture in his eyes. Was he crying? She spontaneously squeezed his hand back. It was a relief when Zach finally released her to applaud loudly at the end of the first half because Amy didn't want Rob to discover that she'd been holding hands with Zach the entire time.

'Let's go for a cuppa.' She shooed Rob out as soon as the lights came up, hoping he wouldn't see Zach. Fat chance.

'Good idea. I'm parched,' said Zach.

Rob swung around. 'What on earth?'

'I've never been to one of these things before,' Zach carried on with urbane smoothness, nodding a greeting to Rob. 'Those kids were really something.'

'Yeah, well.' Rob viewed him suspiciously. 'When did he arrive?' he asked Amy.

'Must've slipped in during the performance.' She didn't elaborate. 'You'd better hurry or we'll be at the end of the queue.'

As they approached the cafeteria, Rob was baled up by one of the parents needing some timber prices. 'I'll get the coffee while you talk,' said Amy. She patted his arm and rushed away, glad to have shaken off at least one of her men.

'What's Thurley doing here? He's not the twins' father. Unless this is your idea of a hot date,' Zach muttered in Amy's ear.

She ignored his jibe. 'His daughter is in the show, too. Teagan is in the twins' class.'

'How cosy. Yet another reason for playing happy families.'

'Zach! Stop it. Anyway, Rob hasn't got custody.' Yet. It had been a difficult issue between her and Rob. He'd wanted to push for custody once they were married, but Amy hadn't been crazy about being Teagan's stepmum. That child had serious attitude problems, but Rob couldn't understand Amy's reticence.

He had a complete blind spot where his daughter was concerned. At least, with her decision now made, Teagan would no longer be an issue for Amy.

'Which kid is it?'

'The little blonde one.'

'I don't want the likes of her influencing my kids.'

Amy bridled. As if she needed telling. 'Don't teach me to suck eggs,' she hissed. She'd been worried enough about Teagan's influence within the classroom, let alone bringing her into the home on a permanent basis. The lipstick issue was a case in point. But it wouldn't happen now, though she wasn't ready to admit that to Zach. She had to break it off with Rob first. She owed it to him.

'If that kid is this precocious at five, imagine her as a teenager. I don't want Emma mixed up with a girl like that.'

'Have your coffee and shut up!' Amy thrust a steaming polystyrene cup into his hand. 'And be careful what you say. The gossip mafia are everywhere.'

'You're a bit tetchy. Been missing me?' Zach's black eyes crinkled at the corners as he blew the steam from his coffee.

'No!'

'Sweetheart, you'd better watch that beautiful mouth of yours.' His gaze fastened on that beautiful mouth. He itched to lean forward and kiss it again.

The beautiful mouth thinned into a cross line. 'I'm going back inside. Finish your drink and go. The kids won't be on again until the finale song so you won't miss anything important.'

Zach shrugged and watched Amy stalk away. In her lilac Indian cotton dress, which flowed around her slim legs, and the black scooped-necked leotard top that gave the impression of being spray painted on to her body, she had the appearance of a ballerina.

She was graceful and elegant. He couldn't wait to be close to her again. He just had to dismantle those prickly barriers she had erected between them and let love work its magic.

In the melee after the concert, Amy pulled Rob to one side.

'I need to talk to you,' she said nervously, deciding to take the plunge whatever the cost.

He took one look at her face and knew what she was going to say.

'Amy, luv . . . ' he protested.

'I'm sorry, Rob. This isn't a good time, but then I don't know when would be.'

They were now in one of the empty classrooms, cocooned from the noise of the concert crowd.

Rob cupped her face. 'Don't say anything. I'll give you more time. As much as you need. I won't pressurise you anymore. Please, Amy.'

'No, I have to get this over, while I feel brave enough. I can't marry you. It wouldn't be fair on any of us; you, me, Zach or the children.'

'It's all because of Morgan, isn't it? He's really got to you.'

'Yes, he has,' admitted Amy with stark honesty. 'But his appearance has also made me face up to my motives for marrying you. I craved stability and companionship. Those weren't sound enough reasons to commit.'

'I'm not a fool, Amy. I knew I wasn't

the love of your life, but I was prepared to take you at any price. I still am.'

'But I'm not prepared to compromise. I'm so, so sorry, Rob. I wish I could have loved you more, loved you as you deserve to be loved.'

He pulled her into a hug. 'There's nothing I can say that will make you change your mind?'

'No.'

'That's a great shame, but I won't give up hope. If things go wrong between you and Morgan, I'll be waiting.'

'No, don't wait for me. If things don't work out for me with Zach, I won't be marrying anyone any time soon.'

15

Leaving Rob, Amy located the twins and they walked the short distance home. She felt curiously light headed and detached from the twins' chatter. Breaking off with Rob was like lifting a huge weight from her shoulders, a weight that she hadn't really realised was there. Was it because she was now free to see how things would go with Zach?

Yes!

It made her jittery just thinking about it.

Zach was parked outside her house in his black Jaguar.

'Mummy, look, isn't that Dad's car?' said Luke.

'Yes, could be.' Her heart flip-flopped and she suddenly felt quite breathless. She hadn't expected to see him so soon.

The twins ran on ahead to greet him. She heard him laughing and extravagantly praising their performances. A rush of tears blurred her eyes. She sniffed them hurriedly away. A rogue drop splashed on to her hand. She hadn't realised until now just how much the kids had missed out by not having a father around.

If she'd married Rob he would have tried to fill that void. But would he have been so thrilled by their little songs and incorrect recitations? Amy squashed the traitorous thought because that was all over, it wasn't going to happen.

'May I come in?' Zach asked over the twins' curly heads.

'No.' The refusal came out of nowhere, generated by pure panic.

'Aw, Mum, please,' said Luke.

'Well, OK. But only for a minute. The kids have to get to bed. It's late.'

'Fine. I'll give you a hand. And then we need to talk.'

'But . . . ' She felt ridiculously

nervous, as if her life was going to change forever.

'Come on kids. The last one to the front door is a — ?'

'Rotten egg!' yelled Luke, taking off at speed.

'Don't get them all excited before bed!' But Amy spoke to thin air. And of course, it was already too late. The children were wound up with post concert adrenaline, excited about it being the end of term, over the moon about going to Australia, and thrilled at having their dad around.

An hour later, with the twins tucked up in bed, Amy and Zach sat opposite each other at the kitchen table. Between them were the remains of an elaborate snack Amy had maniacally prepared to keep her nerves in check. Now she nursed a glass of white wine, more as a courage-booster than because she wanted it.

'You took a big risk coming here tonight. Rob could have been with me,' she goaded and then wondered why she was trying to bait him. What had got into her? Or was it simply nerves?

'Comes back here regularly at night, does he?'

'No, of course not! There's the children to consider.'

'Good.'

'Not that it's any of your business whom I bring back here.'

'But I want it to be my business. I think I have a right to make it so.' Zach picked up the picture Emma had drawn for him. It had *To Daddy Love From Emma* written on it in large, glittery pink letters over the top of a gaudily dressed fairy riding a horse. At least he thought that's what it was.

'I spoke to my mother while I was in France.'

Amy regarded him warily. 'Why?'

'I told her I'd found you again and I asked her about the letters.'

'And?' Amy realised she was holding her breath, wanting Zach exonerated for failing her all those years ago.

'She admitted to throwing them

144

away. She didn't want me leaving while Dad was so ill. And then, when he died, she was frightened that if I took off to find you I might not come back to run the business. She thought she was doing the right thing, under the circumstances.'

'And now? What does she think about you tracking me down?'

'She doesn't like it,' he admitted. 'But she has given her blessing. She knows how important it is to me. How important you are. And she can't wait to meet the children. And you.'

Amy had a sudden flash of insight of how Zach's mother must have felt confronted with the possibility that Zach might have left home and not come back. She felt the same about the twins going to Australia without her.

'I think I appreciate a little of what she must have felt. It couldn't have been easy for her.'

'That's very understanding of you.'

'I think a mother would do anything to protect her family.'

Amy took a sip of wine and decided to change the subject. There was something that had been bugging her since his afternoon phone call. 'So how was France?'

'Good.'

'And the wedding?'

'Great.'

'That was it?'

'The bride looked radiant. The wine flowed. What else do you want to know?'

'Tell me about the company?'

Zach's lips twisted into a ghost of a smile. 'You mean Melanie, I suppose?'

Amy shrugged. Was she that obvious?

'I've told you before, my sweet, you have nothing to be jealous of about Ms Philpot. She's just the daughter of a business acquaintance. Nothing more.'

'And yet you kept it quiet that you were taking her.'

'I didn't know she was coming. It was a last minute thing. After I left you, I went back to the Philpots to collect my suitcase and Melanie was waiting for me, all packed and ready to go. What could I say?'

'I suppose nothing.'

'Not unless I wanted to appear churlish and, after her parents' great hospitality, I didn't want to do that.'

'No, of course.'

'I dropped Melanie off in Paris.'

'Paris?'

'She had friends to see and shopping to do.'

'So you didn't take her to the wedding?' She experienced untold relief.

'No, I didn't, so you can stop sounding like a jealous girl.'

'I wasn't!' Well, maybe a bit!

'Though I don't mind. It's nice to know you care.'

'Hmm.' She wasn't going to commit herself. 'I'm not your keeper, Zach.'

'You could be, if you wanted to.' The air was suddenly charged. Did he mean what she thought he meant? No! Ridiculous.

'If I couldn't stop you straying in the first flush of teenage love, I'm positive I wouldn't stand a chance now.'

'I never cheated on you!'

'You married Chantelle!'

'After you dumped me.'

'You still married her.'

'Years later.'

'Two!'

'You'd shot through, Amy. What did you expect me to do? Go on ice for the rest of my life? I was a young, healthy, red-blooded male with normal appetites and Chantelle was an attractive, available woman.

'Circumstances threw us together. It was natural that we ended up in a relationship. OK, so it didn't work out, but for goodness sake, we all make mistakes. We're allowed to. It's part of growing up.'

He raked his hand through his hair in frustration. 'Your precious Thurley messed up his first marriage, but have you said anything against him? No, just poor old Rob.

'I made the same mistake and married the wrong woman and you crucify me. Where's the justice in that? You're prepared to forgive Thurley and give him a second chance, but not me. Stop being such a hypocrite, Amy.'

'You know nothing about Rob's first marriage,' Amy said defensively even though she knew what Zach said was true. But how could she admit to him that it was easy to forgive Rob because it didn't matter one jot that he'd loved another woman first. But knowing Zach had married Chantelle made her heart shrivel up and die inside.

'And you know zip about mine.'

'I . . . ?'

'What? Do you want all the sordid details? There aren't any. Sorry to disappoint you. It was simply a mismatch. We were too young, too inexperienced. And I was on the rebound. From you.'

'I don't believe you.'

'Believe it, Amy. You sliced my heart in two when you left.'

'I saw you kissing Chantelle! Anyway, it was years ago. I don't want to dwell on it. I have already spent too much of my life regretting our affair and how it ended.'

'I don't. Our relationship was precious. And how can you regret the result of our relationship?'

'I never said I regretted my children!'

'So you admit some good came out of our love?' The dryness of his tone was alarming.

'I love my children.'

I loved you! And still do, if the truth be known. Why was he doing this to her?

'I know you love them, so come with us to Australia?'

His tone softened. 'Please come. You don't have to worry about your work commitments. I have it on the best authority that your parents will care for your home, Linda will clean at the Philpots and Beth will do Thurley's bookkeeping.'

'You have been busy,' she said, feeling the ground being cut from around her and not knowing if she dared to fling

her arms around his neck and tell him she wanted to come with them and that she didn't want to be excluded.

'I have. I'm desperate. I want you by my side. And don't give me any stick about considering Thurley.' Zach slung back his coffee mug, sloshing some of its contents over the table. 'You're not really going to marry him, are you?' he bit out. 'The twins don't want you to and I certainly don't.'

* ★ *

Now was the time to come clean and tell Zach how things stood between her and Rob, that it was all over, but as she took a deep, steadying breath, Zach said, 'Hey, Amy, why don't you give us a chance? I know you're not indifferent to me.'

She felt too shy to say anything, almost too frightened to take the consequences of her confession that she was now a free woman. So much was at risk.

Her whole world was teetering on the edge of the unknown. If she tipped over the edge would she fly high to her ultimate dream or would she plunge into the darkness of that despair she'd experienced when he'd first broken her heart? Would her love be strong enough to hold him a second time?

Zach stood and came around to her side of the table. He picked up her hand and slowly pulled her to her feet.

Amy felt powerless to stop him. They stood only millimetres apart and then Zach slid his hands either side of her head, threading his fingers through her hair and drew her towards him.

His lips skimmed hers. Amy sucked in a breath. Then his mouth was on hers and kissing her as if his life depended on it.

★ ★ ★

Sweet warmth spiralled through Amy like cream in Irish coffee. Her blood began to pound, her heart was fit to

bursting. She clutched hold of his shirt and opened up to him like a parched flower to rain.

Never had Rob's kisses inspired her like this. The years rolled away and it was if she was back in France with Zach, in thrall with their tender first love.

The kiss went on and on and then Zach pulled away.

There was a crooked smile on his lips as he regarded a flushed Amy.

'You see,' he said huskily. 'Not indifferent. I've missed you so much, Amy.'

And she had missed him.

'I finished with Rob tonight. I'm a free woman.'

And then she was back in his arms, being crushed to his chest.

'Not for long, my darling!' he said hoarsely.

'Amy, darling, say you'll be mine forever.'

There was no mistaking the pleading in his husky voice. 'There has never

been another woman like you. I need you. Love you.'

'Love?' she said wonderingly.

'Marry me, Amy Jones. Make my life complete. It's nothing without you.'

And Amy knew with complete certainty that it was the same with her. How could she ever live without him?

Forever with Zach. It sounded perfect.

'Yes,' she said. 'I'll marry you.' And then she was being kissed again and it felt so wonderfully, gloriously right.